Unexpected Nanny

A CHRISTIAN SINGLE DAD SUSPENSE ROMANCE

AVERY WRIGHT

Contents

CHAPTER 1

We Can Do This

ONE

Henry runs and keeps looking back. Everything around him brings back childhood memories of him and his siblings running around playing hide and seek. This is different. Someone is chasing him. He's running as fast as he can, but his attacker is getting closer and closer.

Henry falls and throws his hands up in defense and yells, "Help! I don't know what you want but please don't hurt me."

A blinding light flashes before him and out of the spotlight comes Judith reaching for him.

She lightly responds, "Henry don't worry, I'm here. You are brave and strong, now get up. I'll never leave you. You can do this."

Henry grabs her hand. He just wants to hold on. "I can't do this without you. What if I fail?" Henry questions.

Life is meaningless without Judith. He grabs her hand once more and she allows him. For a moment they sit and hold hands. Judith begins to fade away but just before she vanishes, he looks down at her hands and notices that it's no longer Judith's hands he's holding, but a darker version of hers. He looks into her face puzzled and she smiles as she slowly drifts away.

Henry jumps at the sound of the alarm. It's 5 AM and he feels the tears falling down his face. This has been the same dream for the past two years. What does it mean? Every night like clockwork, the same dream. This is a constant reminder of the loss his family has suffered due to the untimely death of the love of his life, Judith. He must put on a strong face for the boys, but he feels like he's dying inside.

"Ok, Henry," he mumbles to himself. "Enough of the pity party. You don't have time for that."

Going downstairs to make breakfast for the boys and himself, Henry says a quick prayer thanking God for all his help because without him, he would not have been able to make it. Many times, he questioned if he was a good father and if he can make it as a single dad. It was hard but somehow the kids are still alive and happy. What else can he ask for?

After breakfast, the boys run upstairs to get dressed. "Let's hope this morning runs as smoothly as I need it to. I must get to work in a timely manner. Work will be brutal with multiple meetings," Henry thought.

"Boys, let's get a rush on it; we have to be on time today."

As he dropped them off for school, he reminded them that he would be the one picking them up today.

"Don't forget dad, we get out early today. It's Wednesday," Junior stated.

Henry Junior and Jordan Stone sat on a bench in the parking lot of St. Joseph's School, looking around anxiously.

"No, Junior, I don't think we should," said Jordan, the younger of the brothers, at seven.

"It beats sitting here waiting," said Junior, who was ten.

"But Dad's been late before and we didn't walk," protested Jordan.

"Yeah, but then it's on normal days, not a Wednesday."

"Oh," Jordan replied, not understanding the significance.

Junior noticed his confusion. "It means that if Dad thinks school ends at three today, then we have a huge wait 'cause it's only 11:30 now!"

"Ooooh," said Jordan, finally understanding the issue. "But can't we just ask Miss Emsley to call Dad like other times?"

"Aw dude, Dad's probably super busy at the office. We'd be helping him."

"Do you really think so?"

"Of course, he'll probably thank us! And buy us Gino's pizza for lunch and get us Lego toys as well."

"You sure we won't get in trouble?"

"No way dude. Dad'll be so happy, he'll probably wanna take us to the waterpark and even play with us! I'll even tell him it was your idea, then he'll play extra-long with you!"

Jordan smiled at his brother's thoughtfulness.

"That's nice of you, Junior," he said.

"So let's get walking!"

"What about Miss Emsley over there?" Jordan pointed to the tall teacher standing at a distance speaking with one of the parents.

"Let's go quick before she sees us. Her back's turned. Come Jordie, grab your bag!"

And with that, the brothers dashed through the parking lot gate and onto the street to begin their walk home, believing that if it took their father only five minutes to drive them home, it would take them the same amount of time.

TWO

Zoe James stood outside the Conrad Apartment complex. She took a step towards the entrance and then changed her mind, stepping back. She was 30 minutes early, and even though this was a happy event for the family she was working for, part of her wanted this party to be over with. Even though her employers were moving because the husband had a better job, she hated to say goodbye. The idea of letting go was too painful to consider. Turning around, she saw the park over the road and thought it would be better to wait another 15 minutes and then buzz the Bradleys.

Why hasten the tears? she thought to herself.

As she crossed the road, she spotted two boys walking alone and arguing amongst themselves.

THREE

"Where are we, Junior? Dad never drives this way," moaned Jordan, on the verge of crying.

"It's... it's a shortcut," Junior lied. "It's gonna get us home even quicker."

"No, it ain't. It's already been an hour! We're lost!" shouted Jordan, bursting into tears.

"Hey!" scolded Junior. "Stop crying. If people see you crying, they're gonna kidnap us!"

"People are gonna steal us?" Jordan asked, crying louder.

"Yeah, 'cause they'll think we're just kids who're lost!"

"We are kids and we are lost!" cried Jordan.

"No, we're not, and where do you get an hour from?" Junior flashed his wristwatch. "It's only been 44 minutes!"

"Hey, are you kids okay?" asked a tall woman, coming up to them.

Junior looked around nervously. They were alone on the

sidewalk. He saw the entrance to the park and pointed to it. "Yeah. We're just going to the park there to play, right, Jordie?"

Jordan looked at the park, then at his brother, and then at the stranger.

"I want my daddy!" He sobbed loudly.

FOUR

Zoe's heart melted when the smaller of the two boys started crying for their father. It was obvious they were lost. The older brother smacked the younger on the shoulder.

"Stop crying, she's gonna try and kidnap us," he whispered, thinking she wouldn't hear.

She put her hands on the older brother's shoulders. "I promise I won't steal you. Are you on your way from school?" She asked, glancing at the bags on their backs.

The older brother looked at the younger and shook his head to him.

"I understand you're not supposed to trust strangers. And that is good. But you are clearly lost. If you tell me your address, I will walk you to your home, and I promise I'll even walk on the opposite sidewalk. You can just follow me. How does that sound?"

The older brother looked over the road to the other side. He then looked up the street. Zoe could see her idea was sinking in, both sidewalks would basically run in the same direction. If she led them home from the opposite side and they followed her that way, they'd be safe.

"Okay, we're a little lost," he admitted.

FIVE

"Stop that, Jordie," said Junior.

"I'm Zoe. And if he's Jordie..." she jerked a thumb towards Jordan, "... you are...?"

For a while he was undecided whether to tell her his name, but he now knew hers, and she knew his brother's, so... "I'm Junior."

"Pleased to meet you, boys. So, what is your address?"

"Kensington Royal Apartments, Bristol Street, Upper Tribeca."

"Goodness, you are lost. You're going completely in the wrong direction. Okay, if we walk fast, it should take us about ten minutes to get you home, is that cool?"

"On that side of the road, right?" said Junior pointing.

"Yes, of course, young man. Let me cross, then I'll start and you follow, okay?"

"Okay," agreed Junior, visibly relieved.

Jordan nodded and sniffed, wiping away tears with his hand.

Zoe crossed the street, and then waved and started walking back the way they had come. "Hold his hand!" She shouted over the road to Junior, who complied, taking Jordan's hand.

Together, but on opposite sides of the road, Zoe led them home and it took exactly ten minutes.

SIX

At the apartment, Zoe entered with the boys. A friendly concierge, called Sheila, was at reception.

"Hello?" She asked, frowning. "Who are you?" She asked Zoe. Then she turned to the boys. "Where's your father?"

"He forgot to fetch us, Aunt Sheila," replied Jordan, excitedly. "And this cool lady brought us home. I wasn't even scared once!"

"Is that so?" asked Sheila, smiling at him.

"Yes! I didn't even cry!" He added. Junior sighed and shook his head.

"I found them lost in the street and managed to convince them to tell me where they stay," Zoe explained. "So, you know them, then?"

"Yes, they stay here. I have their father's number and will call him to let him know. They can stay here with me in the meantime."

"Okay, brilliant. I have a prior engagement and cannot be late. They will be safe with you?" asked Zoe.

"Safe as can be, Miss. Thank you for your kindness. I never got your name?"

"That's okay. If these little rascals belonged to me, I would pray that someone would bring them home. I was just doing what any other person would do. Them being safe is all that matters. Have a great day." She smiled at the concierge. "Boys, no more walking home on your own, okay?"

"Yes, ma'am!" said Junior, smiling.

"Nope!" added Jordan, waving her off.

SEVEN

Henry Stone was home within 5 minutes after Sheila called him. He got caught up in a meeting and lost track of time. He rushed off to the school, only to find that the boys were not there. He called his neighbor Carol, who would sometimes pick them up when she got her daughter, only to get no answer. Driving home, his phone rang, and it was Sheila. He couldn't believe that his boys had the nerve to try and walk home. His first thought was sympathy for the boys, seeing as how he was the one who forgot that the school closed at 11

AM on a Wednesday, but when he thought of the danger they had exposed themselves to in walking home, he realized that they couldn't just be let off the hook. *If the stranger had not been a kind one but a dangerous one?* he thought to himself.

As he went through the revolving door, he looked into the eyes of the most amazing woman. His breath caught but just as quickly as he saw her, she went out the door and down the street. Sheila had the boys with her at reception when he arrived. Taking them upstairs he firstly apologized for not being at the school to collect them, but then scolded them for risking walking. As punishment, all their devices—gaming consoles, cell phones, and Junior's laptop, were taken away for a week. He also gave them a lecture about the dangers of strangers.

CHAPTER 2
Fun and Sadness

ONE

In their apartment, Henry began setting up his laptop in the dining room to do some work, while he waited for the babysitter to arrive. Yawning, he heard them thundering down the stairs in a race to see who would arrive in the kitchen first. They'd been remorseful for all of ten minutes after their punishment, and now they were their old selves again.

Sighing, he got up from his chair as they tumbled into the dining room, wrestling. The three of them walked towards the kitchen so that Henry could make them sandwiches for lunch.

As they entered the kitchen, Henry's cell phone rang. Looking at the display, he answered the call, with a smile.

"Hey, Mom!"

"Hello, Dear. Home already, or still on the road fetching the boys?" answered Lisa.

"Home. We just got in, so good timing."

The boys took turns shouting 'hello' to their grand-mother, with Junior taking a seat at the kitchen island, while

9

Jordan hopped around his father's feet, shouting hello continuously.

"Jordan, sit down please," said Henry. "Granny says hello to you two as well. She also says to behave yourselves. She says she can hear you all the way from North Carolina." Jordan sat next to his brother at the table.

Lisa chuckled into the phone. "Really, Dear? I said no such thing."

"She also says to listen to me!" Henry added, trying to look serious. His mother sighed again.

The boys dutifully shouted that they would do so.

"If you're busy and need to see to them, I can call later?"

"No, it's fine, Mom. Now is good." Henry walked towards the dining room again but stopped at the doorway. "Mom? Just hold on a sec, please," he said, and faced the boys. "Guys, behave yourselves. I'm just going to chat with Granny in the dining room quickly. Just wait for me here, and I'll make your sandwiches as soon as I'm done. Okay?"

"Yes, Dad," they answered together.

Henry headed off to the next room.

"So," said Junior, smiling mischievously.

"I'm hungry," said Jordan.

"Wanna make our own sandwich?"

"Oh, boy, yeah!" said Jordan enthusiastically. "That'd be awesome!"

"Okay, grab the stuff from the fridge," Junior said. "Oh, get two plates while you're over there."

"Now what?" asked Jordan.

"I dunno," confessed Junior. "This butter is like a rock!" he said, knocking it with his knife. Junior stared at the block as it sat mockingly in its plastic dish. His face brightened up with an idea. "Maybe we can melt it a little bit, so it's soft," he said, excitedly.

"How will we do that?"

"Let's put it on the stove!" He exclaimed.

"That's so awesome!" agreed Jordan.

And so the boys switched on one of the round stovetop plates, and when the plate was warm enough, placed the plastic butter dish in the center of the plate.

They then turned towards the island and began arguing about a comic.

"What's that smell, Junior?" asked Jordan after a minute.

"I dunno," sniffed Junior. "Something smells weird, right?"

"Boys! What are you doing?" Their father shouted as he came back into the kitchen, running to the stove. The boys turned and saw plastic and butter flowing like water over the top of the stove and down the sides to the floor. Puddles of melted butter and plastic were already forming around the stove.

Henry raced to the stove to switch it off and tried scooping the mess into the sink as best he could.

"I think that's where the smell came from," said Junior.

"Yeah," Jordan agreed.

The boys sat at the island eating the sandwiches Henry had made, in silence.

"It tastes funny," said Jordan, abruptly.

"They taste funny because there's no butter on them," Henry explained. "There's no butter because you two almost burnt down the kitchen."

"Oh," said Junior.

The lift bell beeped loudly, indicating a visitor, and both boys jumped up excitedly.

"Becca!" shouted Jordan, as they ran out of the kitchen towards the foyer to open for her.

Rebecca Gillespie, the boys' babysitter, entered the dining room with them in tow. She was 17 years old and the daughter of their neighbor, Carol. They lived in the apartment beneath theirs.

"Rebecca, you couldn't have arrived sooner," said Henry.

"Okay," she answered, coolly.

"Just please keep them out of the kitchen. There's a mess in the sink but just leave it. The cleaning service is coming tomorrow. I should be back by five tonight."

"Okay," she replied.

With his briefcase packed, Henry kissed each boy on their forehead, cautioned them to behave and listen to Rebecca, greeted her with a smile, and then headed to the lift foyer.

TWO

Zoe sat and watched as the well-wishers congratulated Mr. Bradley on his new job. She had arrived just in time for the party. Her sadness was due to the fact that she would no longer be working for the Bradleys because they were moving out of state. Carla Bradley would be a stay-at-home mom and they would no longer need the services of a nanny.

Little Joey rushes and gives me a huge hug around my legs. She could remember when she first started working here. It seems so long ago. Her heart breaks to know that she won't see him again. It feels like her heart is being ripped from her body. She must put on a brave face. Zoe was truly happy for them. Mr. Bradley really is a hardworking man and she has nothing but respect for the way he loves and takes care of his family.

"Well, Joey is super excited about going to a new place. He

thinks we're going on a vacation. I had to really break it down in a way that he could understand that we're not coming back. He is quite sad to see you go," said Carla.

"I am too," I replied. "He's so dear to me and such an amazing little boy."

"That he is, indeed. We are all going to miss you." Carla replied, with tears rolling down her face.

"I'll pay you three months as a severance package," said Carla, at last.

"Thank you, that's very kind," Zoe replied.

"Your severance will reflect later today. We did add a bonus for you. There is nothing we can do to show our appreciation for everything that you have done for us. You treated Joey as if he was your own. Do you have all your personal belongings?" Carla asked.

"Yes, I do. Tell Joey he can call me anytime and make sure you guys send me pictures," Zoe said as she was sobbing and smiling at the same time while walking out the door.

THREE

Henry was the Director and Manager of 2-b-frank, a book publishing company that had been started by his father in North Carolina. As father and son worked together, the business had blossomed into a major publication house, relocating its headquarters to New York. When his father, Frank, retired a few years ago, Henry took over the business, making it into a billion-dollar business.

He'd just gotten to his office when he remembered that he hadn't eaten anything yet. With all the mischief and trouble the boys had been up to that day, he'd forgotten to make a sandwich for himself when he'd made theirs. Sighing, he decided to pop in downstairs for a quick bite.

CHAPTER 3
Saying Goodbye Hurts

ONE

A s Zoe walked home, she saw a quaint little coffee shop called *Chello's*, and decided to stop for a bite. Looking at the menu on display, she saw a little boy walking with his parents on the sidewalk who was the spitting image of Joey. Watching the three as they passed her, she couldn't take her eyes off the little boy as she entered the shop—and collided with a tall man who was exiting with a coffee in his hand. Thankfully, nothing was spilled. Zoe stepped back, embarrassed at her own inattentiveness.

"Watch where you're going! Some of us still have to go back to work!" He snapped.

It was then that she noticed he was in a black suit, with a cream shirt and a black tie with cream stripes on it. It was a look that coffee stains would not have complimented at all. Tall and well built, his piercing blue eyes caught her breath and stopped her in her tracks. To say he was handsome was to rob him of his due. She had always found a man with a beard to be attractive, providing it wasn't an unruly or overgrown one. His beard was neat and short like his hairstyle. He looked to be in his mid-30s.

When their eyes locked, she could see immediately that he regretted his words, and had recognized the harshness in his tone. And yet there was also something about his face that drew her in and made her feel comfortable.

"Ms., I'm so sorry. I was in a hurry and I never should have taken my frustration out on you. Please accept my apology," Henry begged.

To say she was at a loss for words, was an understatement. She could tell he's waiting for an answer but all she could come up with was, "No problem." He nods his head and hurries off.

TWO

Thank you, Lord, that this suit wasn't ruined, was the first thought that had raced through Henry's panicked mind. The daydreaming woman who had walked into him had sadly borne the brunt of his frustration and exhaustion. He realized immediately how rude he had been to a perfect stranger, who herself may have been having an even worse day than him, for all he knew. And yet how could he hope to recover from such a situation with his dignity intact?

As she looked up and met his eyes, however, he was immediately arrested by the beauty staring back at him. She was dark of complexion, her skin reminding him of smooth velvety chocolate. Her eyes, there was something about her brown eyes, something familiar—they literally put a finger to his soul, pausing his very existence.

He opened his mouth to speak and realized just in time that he was about to say something stupid, and quickly caught hold of himself, and gave a quick apology. He sighed, overwhelmed by the vision that stood in brilliant revelation before him.

Looking down at her, as she was a head shorter than him, he wished they could have met under different circumstances. Perhaps in a restaurant or even better, at Church.

Who knows what might have happened? he wondered to himself. And as fast as that thought had broached his mind, convicting thoughts of Judith flooded his mind and he felt that familiar stab of guilt, sorrow, and pain.

THREE

Zoe watched the handsome stranger disappear into the building, wondering if he would glance back at her. In her heart, she fervently wished that he would, but he didn't.

After buying herself a cappuccino and a chocolate-coated cinnamon twist, she took the bus home. She stayed with her two roommates, Emma and Bets, both of whom were nurses at New York-Presbyterian Hospital, or as it was better known as, NYP. When she arrived, she found Emma, who was also her best friend, sitting in her PJs in the lounge on the couch.

"So, how did it go?" She asked, getting up and walking towards Zoe as she entered.

When Zoe burst into tears, she knew what had happened and hugged her friend, consoling her. They dropped onto the couch, holding each other as Zoe vented her emotions.

"Maybe it's for the best?" asked Emma, after a few minutes.

"Nothing," she said finally. "Personally, I think it's better this way. Maybe now you can get back into nursing. You know? Like we all three studied for?"

Zoe sat up, separating from her friend. "I certainly won't be doing nanny work again, that's for sure."

"Well, that's good news. There are openings right now at—"

"And I won't be going back to nursing either," said Zoe, cutting her off. She stood up and walked to the kitchen, where she poured herself a glass of orange juice.

Emma came into the kitchen and closed the fridge door. "Then what will you do?"

FOUR

When Henry arrived home just after five, the boys were finishing off their homework under the watchful eye of Rebecca. She looked annoyed to him, and he knew the likely reason why. He had been taking advantage of her and keeping her from time spent with friends, but what choice did he have? His work was demanding, and he needed a babysitter, and the girl's mother insisted that he use her and not a professional service.

He was going to attempt cooking macaroni and cheese, but after seeing the stove again, he picked up his cell phone, called Gino's Pizza, and ordered a pizza for supper instead, much to the boy's happiness.

"That's so awesome, Dad!" said Junior happily.

"Gino's!" screamed Jordan.

Lord Jesus, give me the patience of Job with these two, Henry prayed to himself.

CHAPTER 4

Drama, Favors, and Chance Encounters

ONE

The next day, Henry sat in the boardroom waiting for everyone to arrive. 2-b-frank was located on the 23rd floor of the Bremicker Building, and they had the entire floor to themselves. He was sitting in the smallest of their three boardrooms.

He was 15 minutes early, which was how he liked it. Better to be early and prepared, than to be late and unprepared. It was a valuable lesson his father had taught all the Stone kids. He looked at the file in front of him. The name on the file was "Robert Morgan."

Robert had been both a successful and frightening employee of 2-b-frank. The file listed many of his achievements over the years, as well as his recent and only offense that had been disturbing and shocking.

Despite the depressing nature of his pending meeting, he found himself thinking of the beautiful stranger from Chello's. He had been incredibly rude and disrespectful towards her, which was not at all like him. If his mother or any of his siblings had seen or heard his performance, there'd have been no hiding from their disappointment. And should his father have seen it? There would be no rock large enough for Henry to hide under—despite his age and his own fatherhood—that his father would not overturn in looking for him to make known his utter disapproval.

He not only regretted his cruel behavior, but also that he would have no chance of ever making amends, as the chances of ever meeting her again were slim to impossible. Then again, if he should ever bump into her again, would he even recognize her? He chuckled to himself quietly. *As if I could ever forget those eyes or that face*, he thought.

"Henry," said Absalom Menze, walking into the boardroom.

He was accompanied by Hannah Rose, Henry's personal assistant. She smiled at Henry as she entered and led Absalom to the head of the table. She poured him a glass of cold water from a water jug.

"Absalom," said Henry, reaching over and shaking the man's hand. Absalom was the owner of Menze Trust. He attended the same Church as Henry, which was how they came to know one another. Menze Trust handled all 2-b-frank's accounting and bookkeeping, since relocating to Tribeca.

Today, however, Absalom was serving as the external adjudicator for the disciplinary hearing that would be starting in the next few minutes. His role was to ensure an impartial verdict was rendered.

"Sad times, brother," said Absalom. "That's all I'll say at this point." Absalom was a man of integrity and honor. He understood that there couldn't be even a hint of bias.

Henry nodded and returned to his thoughts while they waited.

~

Five minutes later, Hannah led Robert into the boardroom. Frowning, Henry looked to her, about to ask a question, but the woman who had been with the company since the beginning and had attended countless such meetings, spoke first.

"Mister Morgan is unaccompanied," she said. "He has declined to bring his character witness with him."

Robert sat down opposite Henry, smiled contemptuously at him, and then did likewise to Absalom.

"Robert, are you sure about this? Having a character witness can only be to your advantage."

"Noted," the man answered succinctly, looking away.

"Okay then," said Henry.

"Right, gentlemen," Absalom began. "The occasion for this meeting relates to a charge brought against Robert Morgan, an employee of 2-b-frank Publishers, who's presently suspended. The charge is brought by 2-b-frank Publishers and Rachel Lee, an employee of the same."

"Where is she, by the way?" Robert asked.

"Due to the nature of the grievance and charge, she has requested to be excused from the proceedings, which I have encouraged, as per the communication sent to you yesterday," said Absalom.

"I see. May I record proceedings?"

"You may," replied Absalom.

Robert then produced his cell phone, placing the device on the table.

"Mister Morgan, for ease of reference, may we refer to you by your first name?" asked Absalom.

"You may."

"Thank you. Henry will be 'Henry,' and you may both feel free to call me 'Absalom.' 2-b-frank Publishing shall be referred to simply as 'the company.'"

Absalom then proceeded with the various legal and compliance details, outlining his duty and authority in the proceedings—that he was essentially judge and jury in this instance, and that his verdict was final and binding. He explained the process for the meeting, outlined the guidelines for respectful communication, and informed Robert that they would also be recording the proceedings.

He then laid out the charges, which related to the violation of the company's standards, rules, regulations, and code of conduct; violation of a colleague's privacy and dignity; theft of sexually explicit and compromising digital material relating to a colleague; and distribution of such material.

Throughout this monolog, Robert merely stared at Absalom, displaying no emotional response at all.

"Henry, please can you explain to Robert in lay terms what the nature of the charges is?" requested Absalom.

"Yes, of course," Henry replied. "Robert, Rachel has accused you of illegally gaining access to her personal cloud account and downloading explicit material—videos and photographs—featuring her in the nude, and then sending the material to the entire office staff, as well as uploading to her own social media accounts. After which you locked her out of said accounts, to prevent her from being able to take down the material."

He paused to give Robert a chance to speak or respond. He remained unemotional and silent, simply staring at whoever addressed him.

"She maintains that somehow you illegally gained access to her cell phone, and in that way, you were then able to access her cloud and social media accounts."

"Thank you, Henry. Has Rachel provided any reason for why she believes Robert would do such things?" asked Absalom.

"She believes that Robert was jealous of the fact that she

had won a recent company competition, which was to design a new banner and logo for the company. They were both in the final running, and the prize included creator recognition and a $5,000 monetary prize. Robert lost, and she believes that was the motivation behind his attack."

"And what evidence does the company have to substantiate the charges?"

Henry then detailed the evidence they had acquired. Emails and text messages had been sent to her where he directly threatened to ruin her and accused her of cheating him out of his victory. Testimonials from three staff members who claimed that he had shared his intentions to "get her" with them. CCTV footage of him placing his cell phone atop hers without her knowledge in the staff lounge and then removing it stealthily before anyone noticed.

Henry indicated that it was the company's belief that it was at that point that Robert had somehow gained access to Rachel's phone. The most convincing, however, was evidence uncovered by Marshall Greene, Henry's brother-in-law, who ran his own successful IT business. Marshall tracked the IP address of the terminal from which the emails, texts, and illicit materials had originated. It was owned by Robert Morgan.

Absalom then detailed the possible verdicts and the implications thereof, and the options available to Robert. Lastly, he gave him a chance to respond to the charges.

"Not guilty," Robert said, smiling.

"Would you care to offer any explanation against the charges, or to refute them in any way?" asked Absalom.

"No, not at all."

"You do understand that if I find you guilty, then not only will you be immediately dismissed, but the company and I are compelled to report this matter to the authorities to initiate criminal proceedings. That means a whole new level of seriousness. You get that, yes?"

"Do what you have to," said Robert, calmly.

Absalom and Henry exchanged glances. Henry didn't like the casual manner in which Robert was responding. He knew him to be a very intelligent, analytical, and cautious man. For him to be this calm, knowing well what was at stake, could only mean that he was up to something. This made Henry very uncomfortable.

Absalom called for a recess so that he could deliberate over the issues. He requested that everyone return in an hour, and he would then have a verdict to render. Robert, however, informed him that they could render the verdict in his absence, as he had a prior engagement, and they were welcome to send the conclusion, and any other correspondence, to him via email.

Despite both Henry and Absalom's protests, he couldn't be dissuaded, and so Henry relented and suggested Absalom do likewise. Robert collected his cell phone and left the board-room, escorted by Hannah off the floor.

Henry sighed.

"What was that about?" Absalom asked, his eyes wide.

"A very troubled man, I believe," sighed Henry again. "Let me give you time to—"

"No, that won't be necessary. It is clear the man is guilty of every charge and that's my finding. I wanted to extend the courtesy of at least going over everything one more time, but the contempt he has displayed for us, as well as for Rachel's dignity, for the company, for the authority of this hearing, and any ensuing police undertaking is shocking."

"It's like he's telling us he did it and doesn't care."

"Exactly, well, once the police are at his door, then he will be caring, I can assure you."

"That's just it though. He's one of the smartest and craftiest people I know. For him to be this calm, tells me that he's up to something."

"What are you saying, Henry?"

"Have we missed something here, Absalom? Something that could unravel all of this?"

Absalom stared at him for a good while. "I cannot see how, but I take your point. Maybe the man is just so deranged that he doesn't really see the danger he is truly in."

"I hope it's that then, rather than the alternative, that he's up to something and we end up with cake on our faces."

When he was in his own office, Henry called Carol Gillespie.

"Hello Henry," said Carol, answering her phone.

"Hi Carol," said Henry, politely. "I am so sorry to ask you and Rebecca, but I'm dealing with a bit of a crisis at the office. If possible, when you fetch Rebecca, could you collect the boys as well? I was also hoping she could look after them until I get home later?"

"Henry, this is becoming far too regular of late. My daughter also has her schoolwork and other obligations, mind you."

"I understand, believe me. I'm just in such a pinch, I really don't know what else to do."

Carol sighed. "I do understand. I know how hard it is as a single father. Okay, fine, I'll talk to Rebecca, and we'll collect the boys. I do think some sort of alternative solution is needed here, Henry. After all, the boys are already spending so much time with myself and Rebecca, you'd think they were my children."

"Oh," Henry laughed uncomfortably. He wasn't sure if Carol was joking or not.

"Of course, that's not an entirely terrible thought, to be honest. Having a woman's presence in their lives is something they desperately need, Henry."

"Oh," said Henry again, but this time, he understood. "I understand. I'll think about a solution, I promise, Carol. And thank you."

"Anytime. You know I'm here for you," said Carol.

"Let me think of that solution while you collect the boys. Please do get them takeout, and I'll refund you, of course."

"No, it's fine, I'll make them something far healthier than that."

"Thank you, Carol. You're a true lifesaver. I honestly don't know what I'd do without you. And the boys love you and Rebecca so much," said Henry sincerely.

Hanging up the phone, he sighed in relief and then thought of the task ahead of reporting back to Rachel and initiating Robert's exit from the company. And then to call the police, and he sighed in frustration this time.

CHAPTER 5

What People Don't Want to Hear

ONE

Zoe had decided to sleep the morning in. After making use of the bathroom, she exited and jumped in fright from seeing Emma standing outside.

"So, what's it gonna be?"

"What on Earth?" exclaimed Zoe. "I thought you were at work?"

"Late shift," she answered.

"Can't a girl even use the toilet in peace these days?"

"You said yesterday that nursing is not an option, so what is your plan for an income?"

Zoe dropped onto the couch and pulled her feet up under herself. "Why is this such an issue? What's going on?"

"I was hoping Bets would be here for this as well, but we swapped shifts. I don't want this to seem like it's all coming from me."

"I'm not following." Zoe said, perplexed.

"You know I hate bringing up painful subjects, but you

were such a good nurse that I hate seeing you give up the opportunity to do something you love," Emma told her.

"I don't want to talk about it. That part of my life is closed!"

"I get it. I'm not saying you should finish med school, maybe something in the medical field. You had a passion for it. You were a terrific nurse. The kids loved you. I know it was stressful trying to work full time and go to med school but maybe if you do one or the other it wouldn't be so bad. Just thing about it," said Emma, looking pained. Zoe could see her friend hated having to discuss such matters.

"There's not much to think about but I will keep an open mind." Zoe responded.

"Yes, and we appreciate that, you know we love you and are always here for you," Emma stated as they hugged it out.

"Well, you can both relax. Just because I'm not headed to nursing, doesn't mean I won't be working. I'll get another job."

"Doing what exactly, Zoe?" asked Emma, her concern was starting to show.

"Anything. I'll start searching first thing tomorrow. I'll find work, whether it's in a supermarket or a restaurant."

Emma shook her head. "Stop playing with me. I mean, what is wrong with you? You spent all that time and money, and did better than everyone else in our class, for crying out loud!" Emma was red in the face and breathing heavily.

Short and petite, Zoe knew better than to allow her friend's stature to deceive her. Emma could be a real hard case when she was worked up. It was one of the qualities she admired about her best friend—her determination.

Emma realized she was worked up and went to sit on the opposite couch, taking deep breaths.

"Okay," she said. "I'm... less agitated, shall we say."

"I'll find work," said Zoe, reassuring her friend. "I know

you guys covered for me when I was without work the other times. This time I got a decent severance. I can cover my share for the next three months, at least."

"Really?" Emma asked, surprised. She shifted on her seat, "She paid you a severance package?"

"Yes. So, until I find work, I'll be fine. Tomorrow, I'll literally scour the street going door to door if I have to with my resume. I had coffee today at some coffee shop..."

She suddenly remembered her encounter with the handsome stranger, and her tummy fluttered. A smile formed around the corners of her mouth.

"What? Hello?" said Emma.

She realized she'd gotten lost in her thoughts. "Oh, yeah, Chello's. I was trying to remember the name. Sorry," she apologized. She could feel herself blushing.

"Looks like more than just 'Chello's' that you were remembering, girl."

"No, it's... I'll apply tomorrow at Chello's. They were looking for a waitress."

Emma stared at her gravely.

"Fine," she said eventually. "I have another proposition for you. You know my cousin has a healthcare agency. They have other positions besides nursing. They are looking for a part time CPR instructor. It's in her office outside of the hospital, so you don't have to worry about being nervous in a hospital setting. I can speak to my cousin, Gina. She said Monday when we spoke that they're short an instructor."

"But listen," she continued. "I really think you need to seriously weigh the pros and cons of not working as a nurse. Don't throw everything away that you worked so hard for. Don't choose the wrong option for the wrong reason."

"Can I choose the wrong option for the right reason?" Zoe asked, smiling at her friend.

"You know what I mean, smarty-pants!" said Emma, playfully pushing her away.

"Will you get the info from Gina for me?" asked Zoe. "So I can weigh both options!" She added quickly when she saw the look on Emma's face.

"Sure," Emma sighed.

TWO

The Stones lived on the top floor of the apartment complex, while the Gillespies lived below them. After parking her car in the parking basement, Carol, Rebecca, and the boys walked to the lifts and pressed the button.

As the lift arrived, everyone boarded, and Carol pushed the floor number for the Stones. Each apartment took up a floor. The lift opened via a thumb scan and code, which each owner had, and anyone the owner granted access to. Henry had granted Carol access, so she entered her code and her thumbprint, and the lift deposited them in the apartment.

"Right boys, off you go. Get undressed, put your house clothes on, and begin with your homework," instructed Carol.

"Maybe you should babysit them?" Rebecca commented, turning back towards the lift.

"Not so fast, young lady," said Carol. She watched the boys disappear upstairs. When they were gone, she spoke. "None of your moanings, little miss 'my time is precious.' We're all busy and all our time is precious. Now you mind those boys. Mister Stone pays you handsomely, and I don't see you complaining when you're spending it."

"Fine!" Rebecca stormed off to the dining room.

THREE

By the time Henry got home, it was almost nine, and the boys had been showered and put in bed already. He was putting his briefcase down and taking out some papers when he heard the lift beeping. Stepping into the foyer, he saw the doors close with Rebecca inside the lift. Grimacing, he took the hint.

When he peeked into the boys' rooms, he looked exhausted and ready to collapse—both boys could see it. They didn't know much of what occupied their father during the workday and knew even less of the current dilemma he was dealing with. But they understood that he worked hard for their safety and future. He told them often enough and explained that as the reason why he couldn't be home as often as they might have liked.

Jordan himself could barely keep his eyes open. He had been fighting to stay awake to see his dad, and having seen him, nodded off almost immediately. Smiling at his youngest, he said a prayer over the boy, and then kissed his brow, before going to Junior's room. Junior was still wide awake and was reading a comic book when he entered.

"Not too late, Buddy," said Henry.

"Yes, Dad. You look really tired."

"I am tired, son. Ready to drop where I'm standing. Catch me if I do?" He asked.

"With my power of superspeed, I'll be there... in a Flash!" He shouted the last word, laughing.

"Not too loud, Jordie is out like a light. Get some sleep, also. Just ten more minutes, then lights off, okay?"

"Okay, Dad. I love you."

"I love you too, Buddy."

"I miss you, Dad."

Henry's heart broke to hear the truth from his son.

"I know," said Henry, bending down and hugging him.

"Soon as this crisis at work is over, I'll be home more often. More of me and less of Rebecca, I promise."

What bothered him was the expressionless face peering back at him from under the bedding, as though these were words Junior had heard too many times before.

"I promise," said Henry again, trying to reassure him.

"Okay, Dad," Junior replied, still sounding unconvinced. "I..." Junior paused as Henry leaned back to say a prayer.

"What—" started Henry.

"... love you, Dad," Junior said, cutting him off.

Henry suspected he had wanted to say something else but decided to rather leave it. The boy would speak when he was ready, though Henry knew that was more of a lie to soothe his own conscience than the truth. He prayed for his firstborn and then kissed his brow. Next, he went to his study and was about to switch on his laptop when the lift bell beeped again for a visitor.

In the foyer, he looked at the wall monitor and saw that Carol was in the lift. Groaning, he pushed the 'open' button to allow her access. She of course had access, and could just enter, but at least she respected their privacy, and 'rang' rather. This was not in his plans for the evening.

Entering the apartment, she smiled warmly at him and greeted him with a firm hug. While he made coffee for them in the kitchen, she took a seat. She'd explained that she needed to talk to him because she was concerned he was overworking himself. She was also concerned about Rebecca being taken advantage of, and the boys being put at a disadvantage under these circumstances.

"At a disadvantage?" Henry asked, confused. "How so?"

"They don't know where they stand. Who's fetching them

today? Who's making lunch and supper? Who's helping with their homework? When will they go to the park again, or to their favorite comic store? Do you see my point?"

"Yes," said Henry, reluctantly. "It's just for now. I have this tough situation at work to deal with and—"

"Henry," she said, interrupting him, "… it's been like this for most of the time you've been staying here. And don't take this the wrong way, but there's only so many times you can use the old 'when things are sorted' line to justify your absence."

"Absence? Don't you think that's a little strong—"

"No, it's not. You spend so much time at work, and even when you're here, you're in your study. The boys need a father who is more present. And they need more of the female persuasion too, a motherly figure is what—"

"I understand," he said, cutting her off this time. "I am doing my best to be more present, and when this situation is over, I *will* be. I'm not just making empty promises." said Henry, sighing. "I know I ask much of you and Rebecca, and I have no right to do so."

They had both finished their coffee, and he was trying to figure out where this was going.

"I know it's been hard since Judith passed, but I think you need help, Henry. You cannot manage this all on your own." As she said this, she reached across the counter, placing her hand over his. He pulled his hand from under hers and gave a weak smile. She smiled at him.

"I am beyond grateful for you and Rebecca, believe me. I thank the Lord every day for you two. Your presence is—"

"I'm thinking you need something more stable than just a presence, dear," said Carol, still smiling at him. "Sometimes, a partnership is needed—"

"A partnership? How so? What kind of partnership?"

"One that works together to help both you and me with our needs. You have a life, I have a life—"

"You're right," interrupted Henry. "I sometimes only see my own needs, but not yours and Rebecca's. You guys also have lives of your own."

"That's not... I wasn't meaning... Look, you have your boys, I have Rebecca, and... What I'm trying to say is, we both have needs that can be met in—"

"You're thinking I should look for a helper? Like a nanny?" Henry asked, intrigued.

"A nanny?" asked Carol, stupefied. "You want a nanny?"

"I see what you mean," said Henry.

"You see what I mean?" She asked, even more confused. "What does a nanny—"

"A nanny is good, yes!" said Henry, excitedly. He stood up, took his and Carol's coffee mugs, and put them in the sink. "Thank you for the chat, Carol. I really mean it. You always help me see things I never thought of." He turned from the sink and offered her his hand to help her to her feet, which she took in dumbfounded confusion. She still had no idea how the conversation had shifted to a nanny.

He hugged her, and with an arm around her waist, escorted her to the lift foyer, where he pressed the button for a lift.

"Thank you, ever so much for this idea. I'll start the search tomorrow!"

"Yes, of course." She smiled thinly. "Anytime. A nanny."

CHAPTER 6

Confrontations, Great and Small

ONE

The lift bell beeped, and Henry's cell phone rang at the same time. Answering his cell phone, it was Walter, another one of the concierges.

"Good morning, sir. Mr. and Mrs. Greene for you this morning," said Walter.

"Let them in please, Walter." Henry said, putting down his coffee cup. He ended the call thereafter. "Boys!" He shouted from the kitchen. "Please hurry and be ready. Aunt Jessica and Uncle Marshall are on their way up!"

The boys shouted with excitement from upstairs. A mad cacophony of sounds then erupted upstairs as they got ready. Seconds later, they came crashing into the little hall at the foot of the stairs. Springing immediately to their feet, they both raced towards the lift foyer, pulling and tripping one another to be first. Henry watched and heard of all this, shaking his head in disbelief.

When the lift beeped the second time, the boys wrestled

each other to push the button, while Henry pushed the button to open the lift.

Marshall and Jessica stepped into the foyer. The boys managed to separate in time to hug each of them, taking turns. Henry shook Marshall's hand and then hugged his younger sister.

"Call Dad, please," she said, separating from him.

"Okay," said Henry. Marshall was being wrestled by the boys.

"Bad brother," she said, playfully punching him on the chest.

"Good to see you three as well," said Henry. Jessica's baby bump so huge it looked like the baby was going to fall out. She looks beautiful.

"Dad's been at poor Marshall all night for updates about that whole Robert Morgan issue."

"Yeah, Dude. I may have to bail you out of trouble on a weekly basis, but I don't actually run the company, you know," Marshall teased, with Junior dangling on his back, while Jordan was wrapped around his leg.

"Hmm... remind me again who had to bail who out, when someone forgot their wallet at home at one of the most expensive restaurants in the city? Who saved my sister from a night doing dishes?" Henry smirked playfully at his brother-in-law.

"I'm never going to forget that night, am I?" Marshall asked.

"I foresee at least another five years' worth of ragging," he replied.

"Lucky me." Marshall laughed nervously. "Let me take these little terrorists of yours to school, so you and Jess can have a quick chat before you both head off to work," he suggested.

"Sure," said Henry. "Sounds good."

~

Once Marshall left with the boys, Henry updated Jessica regarding the Morgan case.

"Dad is really worried about this, and you as well," she replied when he had finished.

"Me? Why me?"

"It certainly didn't help that Mom could hear how stressed you were the other night when she called and how you were struggling with the boys. She told Dad, and he thinks you're being overwhelmed with everything."

"Why didn't he just call me then to check for himself? I'm okay. I handled the whole Morgan situation, and rather well."

"It's not that. Dad feels that you're already struggling to balance everything, and that's why he didn't want to call you directly, and why he calls Marshall for updates. He's scared that if he hounds you with his worrying about this case, it'll just end up adding to your already heavy load of worries."

"You make it seem like I'm in over my head here."

"No, just fighting alone. You need to breathe. You need help, and there's no shame in admitting that or asking for it, Henry."

He smiled at her.

"What?" She asked, uncertain why he was smiling at a serious time like this.

"Funny you should mention that. Carol came over last night to chat."

"About what?" Jessica asked, frowning.

"About me needing help with the boys."

"You mean like a nanny?"

"Precisely what she recommended."

"You sure that was *precisely* what she was recommending, O' brother, you act like you don't have a clue?"

"Huh?"

"Never mind, the advice—if indeed that was her meaning..." And Henry didn't like or understand the giggle and smile that accompanied her statement, "... is sound. Marshall and I said the same thing."

"You did? Since when?"

"What do you mean 'since when?' We spoke to you about it a month ago at the house, when we all got together after the honeymoon!"

"We did?" He asked skeptically.

"Henry, seriously, are you saying you have no idea what I'm talking about?"

"Was that when we spoke about me getting a babysitter?"

"We spoke about you *having* one already—"

"Yes, Rebecca," interrupted Henry.

"Whoever! We spoke about you getting a nanny. You said you had a babysitter already."

"Yeah, Rebecca started soon after we moved here."

"Henry, this is bad. I thought at least you'd have made some effort by now, but you're saying you've done nothing!" Jessica scolded. "And that wasn't even the first time I spoke to you about it. I spoke to you exactly a year ago after the whole Jeremy Halstead fiasco, when you first spoke of moving here. I suggested then that you get help with the boys."

Henry grimaced. "Hmm, okay that does actually ring a bell."

She shook her head. "The whole family is concerned. And this is not like you to be so absentminded and it's not good for the boys, Henry. They need stability and structure."

"You really think that little of my parenting skills?"

"Do not take this as an insult or an assault. You're balancing running a company that has grown exponentially since you got involved. Then you have this catastrophic situation to deal with at work—with a total creep of the same species as Jeremy—and have to contend with raising the boys during all this pressure and time constraints."

"Okay," said Henry, looking dejected.

"Please don't take it personally that the people who love you the most are wanting to help you the most. Remember what dad always said? 'Many hands make light work.'"

He sighed. "So, you all believe I need a nanny?"

"Yes."

"I understand," replied Henry. "I really do. Thank you for your love and concern. It means a lot."

"It's what family is for, silly. I'm just glad Carol planted the seed already. Sort of."

He frowned at his sister.

"In a good way, I mean. Just be mindful of that one."

"What do you mean?"

"It may be nothing, but I have this feeling—"

The lift bell beeped suddenly.

Both Henry and Jessica expected that Marshall had returned and that one or both boys had forgotten something at home, and so using his cell phone he opened the lift and found Carol walking into the kitchen. She entered wearing a nightie, with a robe over it, but the robe was open, and the nightie was tight and left little to the imagination. Seeing Jessica, she quickly closed the robe.

"Goodness, Jessica. I didn't know you were here," said Carol, turning redder than a bell pepper.

Jessica smiled suggestively at Henry and saw that he didn't catch her coy smile. Sighing, she continued, "No problem, Carol. Nice to see you again, all of you," she added with a wry smile.

Flustered, Carol cleared her throat and pulled her gown tighter together.

"You are looking gorgeous," said Carol. "How's the baby?"

"Baby is fine." Jessica smiled.

Carol smiled back and pulled a piece of paper out of her pocket. "Yes, well, I was just stopping by to give your brother this." She handed the paper to Henry, who opened it and read what had been scribbled.

"Elizabeth Adam?" He asked, looking at Carol. A cell phone number had been written next to the name.

"Good friend, and very capable nanny," explained Carol. "Has three grandkids of her own. I thought she'd be perfect for you and the boys."

"That's so sweet, Carol," said Jessica. Carol smiled nervously at the compliment. "And she has grandkids already, you say?"

"Yes, so she has the experience," explained Carol.

"I'm sure she does... have the experience behind her. As a grandmother and all. How old is she?" Jessica asked. "Can she keep up with two boys who are so full of... energy?"

"Well, she is sixty-seven, but a very youthful sixty-seven," answered Carol.

"Well, ladies, I must confess the day is threatening to leave the station without me," said Henry, looking at his watch. "Jess, thank you for stopping in, I do appreciate it, and the chat. I'll leave you to lock up behind you. Carol, I'll join you in the lift, and rest assured, I'll give your friend Elizabeth a call later in the morning."

Henry walked towards Carol and led her out of the kitchen. Jessica followed behind.

"Pleasure, just..." said Carol nervously, "... she prefers to be addressed as Miss Adam," she added. Henry picked up his briefcase on the way to the lift foyer.

"Of course, she does," commented Jessica, oozing with mischief. "At her age, it's only respectful."

"Yes," Carol agreed, as she and Henry entered the lift.

"Love you, Sis, have a great day!" said Henry from the lift. As the doors started closing he blew her a kiss.

"Bye!" Carol said as the doors sealed shut.

Jessica laughed silently to herself. *Oh, Henry, what have you gotten yourself into with that one?*

TWO

After Carol exited the lift, Henry decided to travel by public transport, as he didn't need to drop the boys off. Catching a bus in front of the complex, he jostled down the center aisle towards the back of the bus and sat down next to the window.

Looking out the window, he smiled as the bus soared past all the stationary vehicles on the freeway that were stuck in peak hour congestion. The Manhattan Rapid Bus System traveled in its own bus lane.

Halfway on the journey to work, a passenger boarded and walked towards the back of the bus where he was sitting. When their eyes locked, her face turned white as a sheet, as the blood drained from her cheeks. Seeing the shocked look on her face, he had no doubt that he looked just as shocked as well. The beautiful stranger from Chello's, who'd almost spilled his coffee all over him—whom he thought he'd never see again— stood before him in all her regal beauty and magnificence.

Wearing a knee-length tight black skirt, black heels, and a blue blouse, she looked spectacular. Her hair had been curled, and she had make-up on. Her red lips glistened in a full pout.

As Henry stared at her, he realized he had stopped breathing, and took a deep breath to get his lungs working again. He could feel his heart hammering away in his chest.

The stranger had stopped dead in her tracks, staring at him from the center aisle.

As soon as he was about to speak, his phone rang. He looked at the caller ID, and it was his office. He had to take it since he was dealing with the legal proceedings of his company. He turned his back to her for privacy to make sure everything remained confidential. The call took longer than he expected and when he was done, she was gone. She must have gotten off at an earlier stop. He couldn't believe his luck; this was their second meeting and he didn't even know her name. He couldn't believe his luck.

THREE

Zoe stood in shocked disbelief—twice over. She couldn't believe what she was seeing. *In a city of millions, what are the chances of seeing the same handsome stranger two days in a row?*

But then, shock on top of shock, after seeing her, and recognizing her, he looked away as though she was no one of importance.

Standing frozen in the aisle by both his presence and his indifference, she exhaled deeply. She got a distinct feeling that he wished her to leave him be. Staring at him, her joy in seeing him again, quickly turned to disgust, and then anger at his condescending arrogance. *I did apologize for goodness sake. It's not like the silly coffee spilled!*

Sighing, she plopped herself down onto an empty seat three rows in front of him.

CHAPTER 7
Why God Created Little Sisters

ONE

Henry couldn't stop himself from staring at the stranger in the third row. Even with her back to him, he found himself drawn to her. He wondered what it was about her that called so powerfully to him. It was as if his soul knew hers. He couldn't stop thinking about her. The more he thought about it, the more he realized the only reason he could be so drawn to her was because of how terribly rude he had been to her. God was probably laying that guilt upon his conscience in order to impress upon him the importance of making amends.

What would Judith think of you right now? He rebuked himself. Beautiful, sweet, and amazing Judith, how he loved her, his sweetheart from high school.

TWO

Five years ago, on a cold and miserable night in North Carolina, Judith Stone had been driving home to Wilsonville alone along Gray's Farm Road. After being caught in a very heavy fog, where visibility was non-existent, she collided with another car also caught in the fog, and the two cars rolled off an embankment into Jordan's Lake. The icy cold waters of the lake meant that none of the four souls who perished suffered much. Judith Stone's body, as well as the three bodies of another family who had been traveling in the second car, were fished from the lake the next day. Jordan had only been two years old at the time, and so remembered very little about that night or his mother in general. Junior, however, had been five and remembered both the night and his mom very well.

The police had ruled that the collision had been purely accidental with no culpability on either vehicle driver's part.

At the funeral, Frank delivered a moving tribute about what a wonderful blessing Judith had been—as a wife, mother, daughter, and woman. The family and the world would be poorer without her. In ending his tribute, he prayed that the Lord would comfort Henry and the boys, and indeed the family and that in time, He would allow peace to reign in the hearts of those who loved her most. He also prayed for the Carlson family—the family of the mother, father, and daughter who had died in the second car—some of whom had been present in the service that morning.

THREE

Zoe took a deep breath and entered Gina's healthcare agency. She'd walked the remaining distance from the bus stop to the office. The walk had allowed her to clear her head anyway, and so she didn't mind. The stranger would remain that, though no longer would she think of him as the handsome stranger. From now on, he would forever be known as the *distant and arrogant* stranger. The Bible made it quite clear that as a Christian, she was not to let any unwholesome or filthy language pass her lips, so *Mr. Unapproachable* was his name.

Emma's cousin, Gina, took her right in for her interview. The office was large on the inside with multiple rooms for classes of different sizes.

Gina came across as friendly, but professional. She gave the impression that she was easy-going and approachable, but didn't tolerate any nonsense, and would not accept anything less than your best, which suited her fine.

The pay was decent and she'd taught a CPR class at the hospital before and had unfortunately had to perform it on many patients when she worked in the ER. There was very little convincing Gina needed about Zoe, and so she offered her the position, which would start that next day with an evening class.

Heading back home on the bus, she texted both Emma and Bets to let them know she'd been successful. Emma was working but would be on lunch soon. They agreed to meet up at Duane Park, as they often did, and have lunch together.

FOUR

When Henry's cell phone rang, he looked at the display and smiled.

"Stacie!" He exclaimed, happily answering the call.

"Well, hello there, Big Brother! How is life?" His younger sister replied. Stacie was the baby of the family at 23 years of age.

"Life is going at warp speed, but it's the way I like it! To what do I owe this pleasure?"

"Really?" She laughed. "Come on Henry, you cannot be that clueless."

"Did my baby sister just call me clueless?"

"Yes." She laughed again. "After your meeting with Jessica this morning, you must of course know that the family has been put on crisis control!"

"Are you serious?" He asked, his excitement starting to dissipate.

"You can't blame Mom and Dad, though. After that whole Jeremy stalking Jessica situation, they're determined to ensure all their kids are safe, secure, and supported. So, guess who's coming to dinner?"

"You're in town?"

"I'm at LaGuardia as we speak!" She replied.

"Good grief," scolded Henry. "You could have said something sooner! I would've—"

"Which is precisely why I said nothing, Big Bro," she explained, cutting him off. "Defeats the purpose of coming over to help make life easier for you, you know?"

"And Jessica knew and said nothing!"

"But of course, there are 'no secrets in the Stones!'"

Another one of Dad's life sayings, Henry thought to himself. And yet, how untrue that seemed to be in relation to him right now. He seemed to be the only Stone left in the dark. He would never object to seeing his family, especially Stacie, as he saw so little of her, but didn't like how this was all happening.

"I take it you're going to Uber to the apartment?"

"I've already ordered and am waiting as we speak for a 'Todd' to roll up. I trust I won't be accosted at your apartment by any neighbors with their assets hanging out, right?"

"Clearly you've been at the gossip cabinet with Jessica."

"And I'll be speaking to your neighbor too if she thinks she's getting her paws into my big brother."

"What are you talking about?"

Stacie laughed and then sighed. "You can't be that clueless, Henry? I told Jessica, 'No, he's not that dense!' And then you have to go and sink my ship."

"What are you on about?"

"Never mind, I'll see you at home. I'll get supper going. The code still the same?"

"Yes, everything is the same. I was going to make—"

"Oh no, don't even go there. If I have to listen to my nephew complain once more about the macaroni and puke you make—"

"Macaroni and puke? And here I was about to say I was *going* to make dinner, but figured we'd try dinner at Delicate, your favorite Cuban restaurant, *instead*. But seeing as how—"

"I'm in!" She shouted. "In for Delicate, and coincidentally, in the Uber as well. I have to run... or drive—whatever. I'll see you at home, Big Brother. No working late tonight!"

FIVE

Emma was waiting for Zoe at Duane Park on their favorite bench. She'd bought a large Philly cheesesteak sandwich which had been cut in two. As they sat eating, Zoe shared the good news with her about the interview with Gina.

"That's great news, girl. I'm really very happy for you. You're absolutely sure that this is what you want to do? To work as an instructor instead of coming back to NYP with Bets and I?"

Zoe put her other hand over her friends. "That was not the life I wanted for myself, ever. That was the life my mother wanted for me. I was content with being a nurse, but my parents kept pushing me, especially my mom. I got accepted into med school and finished my first year and worked full time. It was too much. And when she died, I guess I felt liberated from that burden." She lied to her friend. "Please can you accept that and allow me to find my own way in this life?"

"Yes, of course," said Emma. "I understand a little better now and it makes sense why you would want to avoid that profession. Okay then, you know what this means, right?" she asked, smiling.

"What?"

"Dinner's on you, baby!" shouted Emma, and they both burst out laughing.

SIX

Stacie was annoyed with Henry when he arrived home at seven. She'd been expecting him at five already. The boys were sitting neatly dressed and waiting. When their father arrived, they forgot all about their irritation and hunger and were just plain excited to see him. Their father was always in a happier and more relaxed mood whenever one of their aunts or uncles visited and so the fact that Aunt Stacie was staying for almost a week, had them over the moon.

In the car on the way to the restaurant, Stacie kept giving him the silent treatment. Which just made him even more upbeat and jovial as he tried to wear down her defenses, and this delighted the boys to no end, as they tried their best to help their father wear down Aunt Stacie. By the time they arrived at the restaurant, they were all four laughing and ready for a fun family evening.

Jordan was trying to do an Indian burn on Junior, who in turn was trying to show him how to correctly do the prank.

The boys were having a great time. It was so rare that they got a chance to spend with their dad and have his undivided attention. They had placed their order and waited joyfully for their food."

"I have a joke," Jordan laughed as he ate his rice and beans. "What did one wall say to the other wall," Jordan asked.

They couldn't figure it out. Jordan was so proud that they couldn't guess his joke. "The one wall said, I'll meet you at the corner." Jordan laughed so hard he nearly fell out his seat.

"Jordan get up, everyone is looking," Stacie giggled.

When Jordan stood up his face was red and he was trying to gasp for air.

Henry jumped up. "Jordan what's wrong?"

Jordan had tears in his eyes and he was holding his throat. Stacie screamed for help and Henry was forcefully patting Jordan on the back.

Poor Junior was silently praying to God that his little brother would be ok.

"God please don't take Jordie like you did mom," Junior whispered.

One of the waiters came over and preformed the Heimlich maneuver and a piece of meat popped out of Jordan's mouth. Everything seemed to be ok but the manager suggested that they take him to the ER just to be on the safe side.

"Stacie can you please take Junior home and I'm going to ride with Jordan in the ambulance. I want to get him checked out. I would rather be safe than sorry." Stacie agreed and Henry and Jordan were off to the hospital.

Jordan was going to be fine, but the doctor suggested Henry take a CPR class in case something like this happened again. This was something that he suggested to most families. He recommended a class that was near the hospital. Henry decided to sign the whole family up.

CHAPTER 8
It's All About Perspective

ONE

When Zoe saw *Mr. Unapproachable* walking into her class, she temporarily forgot that he was in fact an arrogant and distant man. She just saw the handsome stranger, with his handsome face, and felt her knees going weak again. She could feel the heat rising in her cheeks and knew she was probably wide-eyed with a silly look on her face. Then she noticed his wife and kids with him, and that snapped her out of her fantasy.

An attractive wife, and so young, she thought to herself. *Gross! He's into cradle-snatching. Still, they made beautiful kids,* she thought, as she noted the boys.

Wait, there's something familiar about those faces, she wondered, looking at the boys. But then she saw the handsome stranger's face again, and she forgot all about the boys and the wife. And then she gasped as he playfully tickled his wife.

As they stepped up to the door, she opened it to welcome

them, and their eyes met. She noticed that the wife was at least laughing. She looked at the boys who were also staring at her.

"Welcome to the Wednesday evening CPR class. My name is CPR and I'll be your instructor," she said. The wife was facing her, giggling. Her hair had been tied in a ponytail that dangled below her neckline, but the hair at the top of her head had been messed up from her playful show of affection with her husband. "I'm so sorry, I can't seem to speak tonight, my name is Zoe."

~

"You," said Henry. "Again."

Her name is Zoe, he thought to himself.

Zoe looked at Stacie nervously and then at the boys and then at Henry. "We accidentally bumped into each other yesterday. Such an innocent and unfortunate thing," she laughed nervously. "Nothing weird really about that." She smiled uncomfortably at Stacie.

Henry looked from Zoe to his sister, who looked at him slyly and smiled knowingly. The boys stared, with puzzled looks on their faces. Stacie looked from the instructor to her brother, with the same satisfaction that a cat no doubt feels when watching a mouse running across a room.

"I'm sure there was nothing weird at all, right Henry... *darling*?" Stacie was playing along, pretending to be his wife.

Henry made no reply but continued looking at Zoe. He realized that he couldn't apologize to her now, as it would raise far too many questions. "Yes, we keep crossing paths," laughed Henry, also nervously.

I need to get her alone to truly apologize. Not now, or Stacie will switch to journalist mode and have a thousand questions, thought Henry.

"You keep crossing paths, you say?" asked Stacie, mischievously.

～

Oh no! She thinks I'm stalking her husband! Zoe was starting to panic. She looked at the husband and shot daggers at him. When she saw the glazed-over look on his face, she groaned.

"Oh, just the strangest of coincidences!" She offered the wife.

"Yes, it's not like she was stalking me!" added the husband.

What the...? Stop speaking! She screamed in her mind at him. She flashed her eyes at him to no avail.

"Were you... stalking him?" The wife asked, aghast, pointing a thumb at her husband who stood next to her, pale as death.

"No!" said Zoe, louder than she intended.

～

"Daddy!" exclaimed Jordan. "It's her!"

"I can see, yes," replied Henry.

"The woman who found us on the street when we were lost and brought us home!"

"I said I can see, Jordan... wait, what?" asked Henry, shocked.

"Yeah, it's Zoe. She took us home," confirmed Junior.

"The boys were lost in Manhattan?" asked Stacie, her eyes wide.

～

Dear Lord Jesus, what is happening? Stacie thought. She recognized the boys. "It's true, ma'am, and also, I wasn't stalking your husband, I swear!"

"Brother," added the husband, his mouth wide open.

"Oh, brother, you have no idea," agreed Zoe, wanting to cry. She'd just started this new job and wanted to make a great first impression with her students. And now she'd been given her first unsupervised class, and the first customer is this family.

"Not, 'Oh brother,' honey," said the wife, suddenly. "'Brother,' as in my dufus big brother," she said, and turned to face him. "What do they all mean the boys were lost, Henry?"

"I forgot to fetch them from school and they decided to walk home," said Henry.

"What?" His sister asked, stunned.

"You forgot to fetch them?" asked Zoe, also stunned.

"He forgot to fetch us." Jordan smiled.

"Henry, this is bad!" said Stacie.

"It's not my place, but if I hadn't found them! Imagine if some crazed person had?" asked Zoe.

"Exactly!" said Stacie.

"Look, I feel bad enough, and I promise it was the first and last time," said Henry. "Can we just drop this and begin the class?"

"So, you saw and saved my nephews and have been seeing my brother all over the place as well?" asked Stacie.

"Yeah. What a strange two days it's been. I can't believe you're brother and sister."

The kids were laughing.

"You guys are so funny!" said Junior.

"He's a single dad, in case you were wondering," added Stacie.

"What? Oh, I don't..." said Zoe blushing.

"Stacie? What are you..." Henry asked, stunned. "What has that got to do with anything?"

"I wasn't wondering..." added Zoe.

"Sure you weren't!" said Stacie, smiling serenely. "So... what was your name again?"

"Uh, Zoe."

"Henry, Zoe. Zoe, Henry," said Stacie. "Clearly you know these two rascals," she nodded towards the boys.

"Hi," said Zoe to Henry. *He's a single father. I wonder what happened to his wife*, she thought to herself.

"We will be talking about the 'lost in Manhattan' part later," said Stacie to Henry.

TWO

After getting everyone signed in and seated, Zoe greeted everyone and explained what everyone would be learning so they would know how to react in the event of an emergency. She went around the room and had everyone share why they made the decision to take the class.

When it was Henry's turn, Zoe gasped as Henry explained the choking scene and she could tell how broken he was at the fact that he didn't have the skills to protect his family and not only once but two days in a row. Her heart went out to him.

After class, Henry gave Zoe a wonderful compliment on how well she taught the class. Stacie wanted to know more about their multiple coincidental meetings.

"Like I said we crossed paths yesterday," Henry explained.

"You crossed paths once only and you two are acting like school kids who were caught smoking behind the hall?"

"You were smoking, Dad?" Junior asked, appalled.

Henry narrowed his eyes at his sister.

"See now?" He scolded, shaking his head. "No, Buddy, it's

just your aunt being a journalist," he said, ruffling Junior's hair. "Like I said. We met yesterday, and that was it."

"And this morning as well," said Zoe.

"Oh," said Henry.

"Oh?" Stacie repeated, looking at her brother, questioningly.

"I don't think you saw me," Zoe said quickly, covering for him.

"Wow, it seems you two are fated to do more than just cross paths," said Stacie.

"Stacie!" Henry responded loudly. "Think before you speak! We have young ears present." He flashed his eyes at the boys. "What are you trying to imply anyway? I'm so sorry for my little sister," he apologized, looking mortified.

"Excuse me, Big Bro, get your mind out of the gutter. I meant exactly what I said!" charged Stacie. "You two have now met for the third time in two days, and in a city of millions that must surely have some meaning. Then making things even weirder is the fact that she's the one who found the boys after you lost them."

"I didn't lose them!" He answered.

"I'm simply suggesting that maybe it's meant to be for a purpose. All things work for good, right?"

Henry eyed his sister. "Well, okay then."

Zoe smiled at both of them.

"And that smile?" asked Stacie.

Zoe smiled and her heart went out to the two boys sitting before her. "They're so sweet."

Zoe continued to answer some last-minute questions as the other students were leaving for the evening.

"Might I have a quick word with you, please? I have some questions about the abdominal thrust you were demonstrating." He added to allay suspicions.

"Sure," replied Zoe. However, as Henry was about to

stand up, his cell phone rang. Looking at the display, he saw Carol's name flashing.

"Oh goodness," he grimaced. "I totally forgot to call her friend."

"About what?" asked Stacie.

"Carol was wanting me to call up her friend, who's a nanny." Stacie noted that Zoe's eyebrows lifted at the mention of 'Carol' but practically leaped off her face at the mention of 'nanny.'

Stacie sighed. "That woman is such an interfering nuisance. Yes, I heard. Trust me, we won't be getting an 80-year old woman to look after the boys!" scowled Stacie.

"She's not eighty. She's sixty-something," corrected Henry. The call ended.

"Oh, well, excuse me for making her so much older than she really is," said Stacie, sarcastically.

"What about Rebecca, Dad?" asked Junior.

"Rebecca's this teenager that looks after Henry's kids when he works," Stacie explained to Zoe.

"Oh," said Zoe, smiling at the boys. The boys smiled back. Stacie was staring at her, and Henry wondered what trouble-some scheme was about to be hatched in his baby sister's mind.

"You seem so natural with kids, Zoe," said Stacie. Henry groaned as he realized where his sister was going with that. He looked at Zoe and saw the same recognition. Henry's phone rang again, giving him an opportunity to end this line of conversation.

"I think I should take this. Zoe, can you show me how to get to the hallway, please? I want to take this in private."

"Sure," she said hastily. "Follow me."

Before Stacie could protest, Henry and Zoe went off towards the back of the office. Opening the sliding door, they both stepped out into the hallway.

Henry terminated the call. Zoe frowned.

"Sorry, knowing Carol—my neighbor—she'll call again. I wanted to get you alone quickly."

"Oh, okay," replied Zoe, uncomfortably.

"No, nothing bad," said Henry, noting her discomfort. "I just... I owe you another apology for the horrendous behavior I have displayed. You must think I'm an awful father for forgetting the boys. And then I was so rude to you yesterday, it's unforgivable. I'm not like that, to be honest, and have no excuse. When I saw you on the bus this morning—"

"So you did see me."

"Yes. I'm sorry. I felt so ashamed of myself that I couldn't bear to even look at you, let alone talk to you. But the more I thought about it, the more I felt I needed to apologize again. I wasn't raised to be that way. My phone rang and by the time I was done, you had already left the bus."

"I see," she replied. She smiled, she couldn't help herself. She'd never met someone who was so open with their feelings and so willing to admit their wrongdoing. Not even Emma, her best friend, was capable of such easy confessions. She sighed.

"I forgive you, Henry," she said, smiling. "Forgetting to pick up the boys... sounds like you need help maybe? Maybe a nanny? As for our collision yesterday, I really did feel awful for almost drenching you in your coffee. I was distracted at the time."

"Are you okay?" He asked, concerned. She could sense the sincerity of his concern and interest in her welfare.

She sighed. "I am now."

"But not yesterday?" He pried. She took a deep breath. For a moment, Henry thought she would be unleashing a fearsome rebuke upon him for prying in her affairs.

"No, I lost my job yesterday." She said, instead of rebuking him.

"Oh, I'm so sorry for prodding. That was wrong of me."

"It's fine. I... your sister nailed it though," she laughed softly and unconvincingly. "I was a nanny up until yesterday. And then my employers moved away and no longer needed my service," she said, sadly. "I was heartbroken and distracted when you saw me because this little boy I had come to love dearly was taken away from me forever." As she spoke, tears began running down her cheeks.

"Maybe, if it would help you... it would certainly help me," he said. "We really do need a nanny. My other sister, Jessica, and her husband, Marshall, mentioned it almost a year ago already, that I needed a nanny. And I did have someone, but it didn't work out. Now, I'm using my neighbor's teen daughter, but it's interfering with her schoolwork."

Zoe stared at him, saying nothing.

"It would really help us out."

"You don't even know me..."

"And yet, the crazy thing is, I feel like I do. I feel like I know you or should know you. It's weird. I thought so the very first time I saw your eyes and your face," said Henry, blushing. He realized how dangerously close to being inappropriate he was being.

To attract a young nanny, this was not the way, he thought to himself.

"I felt it too. Like I'd seen you somewhere. And maybe we have, seeing as how often we've bumped into each other." She smiled. "Maybe tonight's not the third time for us to cross paths." She chuckled. "However you look at it, I did feel a familiarity."

"Would you be willing to at least consider the offer? The kids like you too, that much is clear. And Stacie has been all but pitching for you to move in already—as a nanny, I mean! And most importantly, you seem to have a good relationship with God. I couldn't ask for more than if I had prayed to God with a list of requirements."

"I can't. I'm sorry, Henry, but I really can't." She looked away from him, as another tear streaked down her cheek.

"It's because of the job you lost yesterday, isn't it?"

"Yes."

"Because of the boy, you won't get to see again."

"It hurt me so badly." She answered, looking at him again. They stared into each other's eyes. *Would it be so bad to look after this man's beautiful boys? To help him raise them? To help him? To maybe...* She stopped her thoughts from running wild. "May I ask where their mother is?" She suspected divorce, but in her heart knew it wasn't. What sane woman would leave such a man?

"She died five years ago, in a car accident. Well, a drowning," he corrected, seeing the shocked look on her face. Even in the dark, all the blood had drained from her face, making her look pale as a sheet. "It... well, it's a long story." He sighed and looked away. She'd already looked away, in fact, she'd literally moved away from him, and backed herself up against the wall of the yard. "I should head back in before they start wondering where I am," he said, feeling rejected.

She looked down and nodded her head vigorously.

"Are you okay?" He asked, concerned and coming closer.

In the darkness, he suddenly felt her hand on his chest—cold and trembling—and thought first that it was a gesture of affection, but then the hand pushed him away, and firmly. He heard her sniffing.

"I'm fine," she said, her voice trembling.

He understood immediately that she didn't want to be near him, that she wanted to be far from him. He realized that she was feeling overwhelmed. And it made sense to him when he thought about it. She'd lost her 'child' yesterday when she was released as a nanny, and now he'd asked her to take on another emotional attachment, but with two boys this time. And he'd seemingly tried guilting her into accepting the tale of their deceased mother. No wonder she was overwhelmed. He cursed himself in his mind and stepped away.

"I'm sorry, Zoe. I really am, for everything. That was insensitive of me to ask, and even cruel. I'm just not thinking straight lately. I apologize again. Please take your time, we'll be inside. If we're gone before you come back, I just wanted you to know we really enjoyed your class and you're an excellent instructor."

She stood against the wall, neither moving nor speaking. Henry wanted to touch her shoulder but knew that would be unwise. Instead, he headed back inside the office.

CHAPTER 9
An Unexpected Surprise

ONE

At the end of her classes, Zoe was waiting for Tony, who was partners with Gina. He always offered his female staff lifts home after the evening classes. He mentioned to her that he was familiar with the Stone family. Henry created and made posters and flyers for the healthcare center. She sat by herself while waiting for him to return from dropping the first four ladies. There were three left, including her. While waiting, she thought about the events of the last two days and the implications for her. She couldn't deny that God was at work in these events, carrying out His purposes for her and her future. Of that she was sure. But knowing that God was at work didn't absolve her from making the necessary choices. And that was where she came to a crossroad. What was the right choice for her to make?

She'd continued watching the Stone family for the remainder of their class time, and she could see that as the evening carried on—as the boys laughed and had fun, as her own mood and spirits lifted, as Stacie joked and teased everyone, and they all ended up enjoying themselves—that Henry was happy again. She could see in his face how relieved he was to see her smiling, as well. And why did it matter so much to her that Henry was happy and noticed her? Obviously, she knew why, who was she kidding? *But that was such a delicate situation*, she thought to herself, *to be handled with care.*

She had to make a decision. Two paths had been put before her, one by her own designs and one by God's. She'd set forth the path of working at the healthcare office, while God had set the path of working as a nanny again for the Stone family. It was an impossible task, one that she didn't know if she had the strength, courage, or the subtleties needed to pull off. And yet, the more she thought about it, the more obvious what choice was the correct one and what God expected of her. When Tony arrived to collect her, Gina and Elsie, she asked him for a favor.

TWO

In the car, as the boys slept, Stacie scolded Henry for being irresponsible with their safety, and again stressed the importance of getting help. He agreed and promised her again that it would never happen again. He then updated her about his conversation with Zoe and why she wouldn't be accepting the nanny offer. He spared Zoe the indignity of going into too much detail about her emotional state, but Stacie understood and accepted her decision.

When they arrived at the apartment, they each carried a child to their bed.

Stacie was annoyed with Carol's constant interference and threatened to have a word with her in the morning, but Henry forbade her from doing so, explaining that Carol was just a well-meaning friend who sometimes took things a little too far. In any event, while the age of Carol's friend all but discounted her as nanny potential, it did allow them the option to employ her as a temporary measure until they could find a full-time nanny.

That evening, Stacie and Henry sat in the living room reading.

"I really do believe that you're doing the right thing Henry in getting a nanny," said Stacie, putting down her book. "Mom and Dad will be thrilled; I promise you that. Just please say nothing about the boys walking home!"

"I wasn't planning to, Stacie. Anyway, I had toyed with the idea for a while since Jessica raised it with me last year, but I guess I procrastinate a little too much."

"You excel at so much, it's nice to see there is at least some area you're weak in."

"And of course, there is the park bench over the road for you to spend your week on while in the city. I'm sure your luggage will be super safe there, as well."

"Someone's getting cranky in their old age. Do you need your food blended as well, for easy eating?" Stacie laughed.

"Ouch," said Henry. "Look, jokes aside, I know I need a nanny, and I'll get one. I'll use Carol's friend until I can find the right one, providing she's not wheelchair-bound or some sort of geriatric ax murderer. I know how busy you are with work, and so refuse to be the reason you miss out on the next big scoop."

"Well, I've looked into some agencies and maybe Monday you can take the day off and we can go visit some of them?"

Henry inhaled deeply and looked away, smiling thinly. Stacie recognized the smile. It was his polite way of saying he was not happy about something but didn't want to actually say that.

"Look, I know it's important and a priority, but Monday has way too many issues to sort out at work with the Morgan case. We're handing over our files to the police, and—"

"Fine, I get that it's important. Can't it be postponed to the next day? Or maybe rope Dad in? He won't mind, you know he'd love to be in the thick of things again. Plus, our old man will do anything to see the boys again."

"Stacie, what's with the pressure? I told you I'll do it and that I understand the importance."

"A year, Henry. It's been a *whole* year since Jessica first spoke to you about it after Jeremy. She told me all about your conversation this morning. You really forgot to do anything? I mean, can't you see how unlike you this all is? You're normally the first person to come running when one of us needs any help, which is really annoying since *I'm* trying to be the favorite child. You're ruining my chances, Brother!" She shook her head dramatically at him.

Henry looked at her and then shook his head also, laughing. "Honestly, I wish Mom would fess up that she dropped you on your head as a baby. Numerous times."

Hissing at him, she continued her actual point, "And now when you're the one who's in need, you do nothing and want no help."

"I got Rebecca—"

"That's a bandage on a broken arm. Jess and Marshall spoke to you again at Mom's last month, and you did nothing since then. You didn't even remember the conversation, Henry. Can you not see how overwhelmed you are, that you even forgot!"

"Okay," Henry said softly. "Okay."

"I'm not trying to make you feel bad or hurt you. I'm just saying that this is serious. I love you, Bro. I'd catch a grenade and all that. But this needs to be sorted for your sake, and the boys'. Those poor kids are shuffled between you, Carol and Rebecca. Junior told me while you were outside with the Zoe, that he doesn't even know sometimes who's fetching him— you or Carol."

"He said that?"

"He said he prefers Carol because she's at least on time. Most of the time when you come, you're late. And hearing about their walk yesterday, I can now understand why he says the school often needs to call you to get them."

Stacie reached over to Henry and touched his hand. He covered it with his hand. "I'm not saying you're a bad father, so please don't even think that for a second. You're a father in the same mold as dad. I'm just saying he had Mom to help him, and a lot fewer work issues and commitments. You need to balance out work and you need a nanny. And you need one yesterday already."

Suddenly, and conveniently, Henry's cell phone beeped, indicating a new text message had just been received. Stacie released his hand so he could retrieve his cell phone. Taking it from his pocket, he saw that the message was from an unknown number. Opening the text, he read the message.

"Oh," he said.

"What is it?"

"Listen for yourself. 'Hi, Mister Stone. It's Zoe James. I hope you're well. Sorry to message you so late, but I've been thinking about your offer. If you're still interested in me as a nanny, please do feel free to respond at your earliest convenience.' Wow," added Henry. "This changes things."

"It does. How did she know our surname is Stone though? We never told her that," said Stacie, intrigued.

"Are you sure? We must've."

"Unless you told her when you two were outside. For that matter, where did she get your number from?"

For a few seconds, Henry looked puzzled, then he smiled. "Tony. She must have asked Tony for my details. He probably still has it from when we did their marketing supplies for them."

"Okay," said Stacie. She stared at him. "Well?" She asked,

lifting her hands in a questioning gesture.

"Well, what?"

"Are you going to call her or not?"

"But it's after 10? Isn't it late?"

"She just texted you a minute ago. Do you think she fell asleep a minute later?"

"Oh, good point."

THREE

It had been almost five minutes since Zoe received confirmation that her message to Henry had been received and read. She suspected that he probably felt it was late and would call in the morning. It did disappoint her knowing that he wasn't as excited as she'd expected him to be to talk to her. Secretly, she hoped that he would've called her immediately. She didn't think there had been anything antagonistic or troublesome in the message she'd sent, as she'd spent the better part of ten minutes typing and retyping it. He was probably being respectful or was tired and would call tomorrow. She put her phone down on the pedestal next to her bed, switched off the lamp, and rolled onto her side, facing away from the pedestal.

Her cell phone rang. She saw "Henry Stone" on the display—a name she'd added to her phone only 30 minutes earlier. She took a deep breath and then answered the call.

The call lasted barely three minutes. Henry was thrilled to know that she'd changed her mind and he would be happy to meet at her earliest convenience. He asked how she'd gotten his cell number and didn't seem at all surprised when she said she'd asked Tony. They agreed to meet the next day, which was Saturday, at 10 AM She thanked him for the opportunity, and he again thanked her for reconsidering. They ended the call.

"Please be doing the right thing," she said out loud to herself.

CHAPTER 10
A Meeting at Kensington

ONE

Zoe woke Saturday morning, refreshed and excited for the day ahead. She was nervous about her interview, but also supremely optimistic that this was God's will. Either the meeting with Henry would be a success and she'd be the new nanny, or if not, she would be at her class later that day.

When she arrived home the previous night, Emma had been waiting for her to see how her first day had gone. She told Emma everything about her first class, except about the Stones and the potential nanny gig. She felt it better to wait and see what happens.

She hopped out of her bed and went to the bathroom to freshen up and dress for the day. After washing her hair, she blew it out to dry and style it, deciding to leave it loose. She opted for a casual look and dressed in blue jeans, a white sweater, and flats. In the kitchen, she made breakfast for herself. Warming milk in the microwave for her oatmeal, she saw Emma had left a note for her, along with some cash in an envelope to bring supper home for all of them from the restaurant.

My favorite restaurant, she thought to herself smiling.

She left the apartment just before nine and headed to the bus terminal. She'd be early for her appointment, but that was fine. She'd rather be early than late. As she knew where the apartment complex was already, she planned to be there by 9:30 AM promptly.

TWO

Henry was in the kitchen making himself a cup of coffee when his cell phone rang. The boys were in the lounge watching cartoons. Stacie, who had always been a midday riser, was still in her room, presumably fast asleep. Grimacing, he reached for his phone, expecting it to be Carol with a tongue-lashing prepared. He was surprised to see that it was reception instead. He looked at the clock and saw it at 9:30.

Answering the call, he was pleased to know that Zoe was that keen on working for him, but was equally impressed that she was that early.

The early bird catches the worm, he thought to himself. He asked Walter to send her up straight away.

He started making a second cup of coffee for her while waiting and thought about their conversations the previous night. She'd gone from not being in the least interested in being a nanny to his boys—she even seemed pained by the thought—to suddenly being keen and willing. It was strange, and he would ask her about that. Maybe she was more cautious, and not given to making decisions on a whim. Maybe she'd just needed time to ponder the offer? He'd definitely need to hold off on the details about Judith and the accident. He didn't want to come across as trying to guilt or manipulate her in any way.

That detail had definitely unsettled her the most last night, he thought to himself, *though it clearly must have worked as she did end up reconsidering.*

The lift bell beeped. Walking over to the lift foyer, he didn't check the monitor as he assumed that it was Zoe in the lift. Opening the lift, Carol stepped out. And she didn't look very pleased with him.

THREE

"Aah," said Walter to Zoe. She thought he was delightfully sweet and helpful. "There we go, the lift should come now. "Must be a glitch," he said.

"A glitch?" She asked.

"Yes, it seems to have gone to Mr. Stone's apartment first before coming here. Unless maybe he's coming downstairs to collect you personally?"

"Oh," said Zoe, suddenly flustered.

The lift arrived and opened and was empty.

"Oh," said Zoe, disappointed. She stepped in, and Walter wished her well as the doors closed. He'd explained to her that each apartment unit took up an entire floor and that Henry's apartment was on the top floor. When the doors opened, she'd be in his actual apartment.

As she neared the top floor, according to the lighted buttons on the pad, she could hear muffled voices. As the doors opened, she saw Henry—wearing jeans and a T-shirt with sneakers, talking to another lady—a very attractive one—wearing a yellow dress and yellow pumps.

"... honestly Henry, I'm trying to help you and the boys, to get more stability in the home and Miss Adam is perfect for that. All you need to do is—" The lady turned to face Zoe, "Yes, yes, come in," she said. She looked back to Henry. "Is she here to collect something?"

Henry looked at Zoe and then at Carol, with a puzzled look on his face. "Collect something? I'm not following you... do you mean Zoe?"

Zoe stepped into the apartment.

"Zoe?" asked the lady in the yellow dress. "Who's Zoe?" She asked with unveiled disdain, looking her up and down from toe to top.

"Hi there," said Zoe, extending her hand to the lady. "I'm Zoe."

The woman looked at her hand but made no attempt to take it. She looked at Henry. "What's going on? Who's this woman? I thought she's a courier of some kind, by the way she's dressed." The woman looked back at her, giving her yet another once over.

"Good grief, Carol. No, not at all. This is Zoe. She's here about the nanny position."

"What?" Carol exclaimed loudly and in shock. "What about Miss Adam?" She demanded, looking aghast.

"I feel she's a little advanced in age for such young boys, so Zoe is my preferred choice."

"Your preferred...?" Carol looked like she was about to suffer a stroke. "Henry, I already told Elizabeth about the job and assured her—"

"Now, Carol," Henry said firmly. "I'll choose who's ideally suited for the needs of my boys. I appreciate your advice to get a nanny. It was good advice. And here is my perfect candidate, if I must be honest. Now, I appreciate all your concern and assistance, but I need to get this meeting underway. I hope you have a great Saturday morning." He reached between the women and pushed the lift button, which opened the doors again, as the lift hadn't yet departed.

Carol gave Zoe the once over again and then entered the lift in a huff. She pushed the button, and the doors closed with her sending daggers at Henry.

FOUR

"I hope I haven't caused you any trouble." Zoe said anxiously.

"No, not at all. Carol's the neighbor. You'll see a lot of her. She's just very concerned about the boys and feels I need the help. I think she sees me as a terrible father."

"I never saw a terrible father last night. Quite the opposite, actually."

Henry smiled sheepishly and scratched his head. He was turning bright red.

"Apologies if that was out of line though. I only meant it sincerely."

"I'm sure you did, and don't apologize. My family does tend to agree with Carol though." He said.

"About what? Being a terrible father, or needing help with the boys?"

Henry smiled. "Fair point. About needing help."

"I'd think so, yes. What I saw last night was a father who's very caring and concerned about his boys and willing to do whatever is necessary to ensure they are taken care of. And your sister seemed to see you in the same light."

"Stacie's still asleep. I hoped she would join us, she might still. She's really not a morning person, I dare not wake her."

"It's fine. I can either wait until she wakes or come back another time to meet her. I'm easy." Zoe gasped and closed her eyes. "Easy-going... is what I meant to say," she added, blushing terribly herself.

"Easy-going is what I heard," added Henry shyly. "No, let us get started, if she wakes, then she can join us. And if she sleeps, then she misses out. It's my choice in any event. She's only here for a few days." Henry led her to the dining room.

"Oh, so she doesn't stay with you?" she asked, trailing him.

"No, she mostly stays with our parents in North Carolina. Otherwise, she travels all over the planet. She's a journalist."

"Of course, I should have guessed. Stacie Stone. She writes for the New York Tableaux."

"Yes, that's right." They entered the dining room, and Henry pulled a chair out for her to sit on. "I was making coffee for us when Carol came in, would you care for some?"

"No, thanks," she replied.

"To the coffee or Carol?" asked Henry, laughing. He held his hands together, apologetically. "That was terrible of me."

"Neither, please," she added, smiling.

Henry smiled and nodded. "She does mean well though."

"I don't think she'll be happy if I get this position," she said.

"No, don't think that way. She's sweet. Just very... involved..."

"Yes, I could see that."

"She would like you just fine."

"I think Henry, if you will forgive me saying so, as a woman, I can tell you that she would not be happy, and you should be aware of that should you choose to appoint me. I wouldn't want to come between you and your... lady friend," she explained.

"Well, she's just a friend, nothing more. But I really don't know what to say to that. I'm not sure why you would think she wouldn't like you..."

"Because she sees me as..." she sighed and looked away.

"Please speak freely."

"Okay. I'm being very blunt and probably it's not my place, but I do like you and the boys. I like this job and would want to take it with both hands. I'm sorry about my reluctance last night. Having said that, I don't want to take a job and then be dismissed a week later because your neighbor doesn't care for me."

"Aah," replied Henry, understanding her concern. "I see why you would be afraid of forming a bond with the boys and then being dismissed. That won't happen here, I promise you."

"You can't really promise that though, you don't really know me. You may not like me *yourself* after a week, not because I'm a horrible person, but we just may not be compatible."

"Oh," replied Henry, surprised by her statement.

"I'm not trying to talk you out of employing me, I promise." She smiled. "I just mean, of all the reasons to dismiss me, that I cannot control, your neighbor is the more concerning one."

Henry sat down opposite her at the table.

"I think we would get along fine, honestly, I believe that with all my heart," she assured him.

"I agree," he added.

"I try not to get involved in my employer's personal affairs," claimed Zoe.

"I see." And this time, he truly did understand. "What is it that you 'see?' And please be frank with me, it's fine."

She sighed. "She likes you... your friend. She likes you romantically."

"What? Carol? No, you must be mistaken and if she did, the feeling is not mutual. I make decisions in this house and what others think does not affect me," Henry laughed.

"Forget it, sister, you're talking to the blind and departed," Stacie chirped in from the doorway.

CHAPTER 11
Mutual Arrangements

ONE

"Good luck with that," Stacie laughed as she came in and sat down next to her brother. She stared at him and shook her head. Zoe smiled.

"What are you two talking about?" asked Henry.

"That woman has been after you since the day you moved in here," said Stacie. "Everyone knows it, how can you not?"

"No," said Henry, looking at his sister, frowning.

"My big brother here is so oblivious that Judith, his late wife, had to approach him to ask him out. And he was stunned for a week to find out she even liked him, I kid you not."

Henry looked flabbergasted. "Are you guys serious?"

Zoe nodded shyly.

Stacie noted that her confirmation seemed to have settled the matter for her brother. Zoe looked at Stacie and saw she was staring at her. Zoe smiled nervously, and then Stacie returned the smile warmly, setting her at ease.

"Okay, well, I assure you, her feelings have no impact on

this decision. And about the decision, you said, 'if I should choose you.' There is no *if* about this Zoe. I only asked you over to get to know you a bit better." He looked to Stacie, who smiled back.

"I'm convinced that you're the perfect person. I believe God has intended for us to meet and for you to be here."

"Thank you for your trust and confidence. I am very pleased and grateful for this opportunity. You have no idea what it means to me," she said.

"Well," said Henry, sitting again. "Tell us about yourself and then we will," he said as both women sat again.

And so Zoe shared details about herself with them, those that she felt were relevant and important to share. She didn't tell them everything, and nor did she tell them what was probably most significant for them to know about herself and her history. She felt that sharing that information might deny her the opportunity that had just been gifted to her.

TWO

Stacie loved stories, especially biographical ones. As a journalist, stories were her bread and butter, after all. So when she listened to Zoe's life story, she listened not just as someone hearing an interesting story, but as a journalist.

Zoe James had grown up in North Carolina as well, which surprised and pleased the siblings, with Henry bombarding her with questions about her experiences growing up in North Carolina. She'd lived in Newhill, which wasn't far from Wilsonville, where the Stones lived. She spent a great deal of time talking about the James' of Newhill, and then diverted almost seamlessly to her time at Chapel Hill Nursing School at the University of New York. Stacie detected that little misdirection immediately, which mildly intrigued her. She attributed Zoe's reluctance to talk about her immediate family

—her parents and any siblings—to a possibly unhappy home life. The focus on the extended family did suggest that also, and her implying more time spent with them rather than the immediate family made sense in that light, Stacie thought.

Zoe studied nursing, as her mom believed that would be a good career path for her. She graduated with a Bachelor of Nursing degree. She went on to complete the first year of med school but realized that wasn't the correct path for herself. Stacie's interest in the misdirection peaked with the contradictory details about the role of Zoe's mother in her life. For someone who had said virtually nothing about her birth parents when telling about her childhood, her mother had an oddly pivotal role in her studies and career choices.

She decided to pursue different career options, eventually working as a nanny. Stacie frowned as she listened to the mother being relegated once again to unimportant status. *Something happened to the mother, or both parents, that had a major impact on this woman's life*, she thought.

She worked as a nanny when she could, otherwise, as a waitress at various restaurants. She described herself as friendly, warm, sincere, honest, open, and dedicated. She'd given her life to the Lord 15 years earlier and was a devoted Christian. She'd dated only once in her life, and that didn't go well. She only had two good friends in the city, with whom she lived.

THREE

Zoe took a deep breath after finishing.

Stacie stared at her, her mind working and processing the information that had just been shared with them.

"Imagine that, we might have driven past each other countless times on the freeways." Henry laughed.

Zoe smiled uncomfortably at that.

"I guess all that's left is for me to tell you what I need from you, what the pay structure is. Then you need to tell me whether that suits you. If yes, then you need to tell me when you would like to start," said Henry.

She would need to arrive in the mornings by 6:30 AM to get the boys up and ready for school with breakfast by seven. She would then drive them to school. Henry had two cars, so she could drive the second. He confirmed that she had a driver's license. She would then have free time—as much as she needed—and could do as she pleased, providing the boys were fetched when school was done, that lunch was ready for them when they arrived at home, and that they were helped with homework. He didn't mind if she used the car for personal reasons either.

She was responsible for the boys' activities in the afternoon, and also needed to ensure supper was ready for the family. She was welcome to partake in their meals with them, including breakfast, or take them home if she preferred. Her day ended at five. If Henry worked late, then he would pay her overtime. She may need to work the odd Saturday as well, should he have to work. In terms of compensation, he would provide her with medical insurance, and the wage he offered was almost double what she'd expected.

"Wow," she said when he stopped speaking.

"Is that a good or a bad 'wow?'" Henry asked and Stacie smiled at her.

"That was a definite good wow. That's very generous of you, Henry," she replied with a smile. "If I may still call you Henry. When we met yesterday... well, when we officially met," she giggled, "It wasn't as an employer and employee."

"I'll continue being Henry if you continue being Zoe."

"I graciously accept, Henry." Zoe agreed.

"When do you think you can start?"

"Well, I think tomorrow would be best. I think I'd be in a

little trouble with my roommate, whose cousin owns the place that I teach. I'd probably be in trouble with Tony as well if I just suddenly dropped him."

"Deal," said Henry. "So, we now know you, but you don't know us. Let me give you some details about the Stones."

FOUR

The Stones grew up in North Carolina in the little town of Wilsonville. Frank and Lisa had four children, Henry the eldest, then Jessica who's married to Marshall, William, and lastly, Stacie. The Stones are a very close-knit family, who make the necessary time to see one another and check in regularly. They were raised in a God-fearing home with constant love and laughter. They were taught to be there for one another and the importance of family. Frank, started his own publishing business, called 2-b-frank, which Henry now runs since his father retired. Jessica was also a journalist like Stacie, while her husband, Marshall, owns his own IT company. There expecting their first child. William is the jokester in the family. Henry briefly spoke about his late wife, her accident five years ago, and how he and the boys have been faring ever since.

FIVE

"Any questions or anything you'd like to ask?"

"Nope, I'm actually all good. You've told me all I need to know," said Zoe.

"Well, I think Monday, we can do a test run and get you familiar with the day's routine. I suggest that you drop the boys at school and myself at work, that way you can see where work and school are. After dropping me off, you can test run your morning to see what you want to do during your free time. I mean, you can use the car to drive home if you like—it's all up to you."

"When I leave," added Stacie, "You would of course be free to use the spare bedroom yourself if you don't feel like going out or going home but do want some privacy."

"That's sweet, thank you," said Zoe.

"Then fetch the kids from school and I'll make my own way home," said Henry.

Zoe nodded and smiled.

"Okay, then I guess we covered everything. Let me walk you out then," Henry said.

Zoe said goodbye to Stacie and then followed Henry to the lifts. She was surprised when the lift arrived and Henry got in with her. On the way down, he had another question for her, one she'd expected.

"What changed your mind? I thought you were lost to us for sure."

"I suppose the providence of it all, spoke volumes for one."

"I have to agree on that. God has clearly been busy putting us together, it's a hard fact to ignore."

"Totally," she agreed. "And then seeing you and the boys together. Seeing the love, the closeness, the spirit you all three have. It was a done deal. I also tend not to just jump without first looking long and hard." The lift opened and they entered the arch, walking towards reception.

"I could tell you put a lot of thought into this. I am grateful for whatever changed your mind."

"You're most welcome." She smiled.

At the reception, Henry arranged for Walter to scan her thumbprint for the biometrics. Walter laughed and congratulated her. He generated an access code for her as well, of her own choosing.

Henry then wished her a pleasant weekend and said that

he was looking forward to her return on Monday. She agreed and said the same. As they stood at the entrance to the complex, Carol drove out of the parking basement. She looked in their direction, and as both Carol and Henry lifted their arms in unison to greet, she looked away and drove off.

SIX

Later that day, the Stone family had their weekly catch-up video conference call. It was something that Frank had suggested after the Jeremy incident, which everyone had agreed to. While great effort was made to attend the call every week, everyone was more than understanding when someone couldn't make the call. Today, William had a prior engagement that couldn't be shifted and so he'd excused himself. A major point of discussion was of course the nanny situation.

"I just wish everyone hadn't felt so reluctant to speak directly to me about their concerns," Henry was saying.

"Hello? What exactly have I been doing, and quite a few times also, if I may say!" Jessica snapped.

"Yes, but I just meant like, Dad, you shouldn't have felt that you couldn't share your concerns about 2-b-frank with me, or your concerns about my wellbeing either."

"Yes," agreed Frank, "But my worry was I'd overload you or make you feel even more stressed. But you're right. I should've just done so. I promise that it won't happen again."

"Bottom line is, there's now help in place from Monday onwards at home with the boys, so now we just need to get Henry sorted at work," Stacie added.

"Yes," said Lisa. "I don't want to have to be the middle person all the time between your dad, and you, Henry."

"Now, Honey," said Frank. "We already sorted that out. So that won't happen again."

"But what about this Robert character?" Lisa asked. "It's like Jeremy all over again."

"This is worse than that, Mom," said Jessica. "This scumbag actually shared nude pics of that poor woman. He makes my blood boil!"

"Look, it's going to the cops on Monday, and then they take over. So it's a closed case for us—" started Henry.

"And then I expect to see you setting yourself strict business hours, son. Hours that you will abide by, is that understood?" His dad added.

"Yes, Dad." He looked irritated.

"Don't 'yes, Dad' me with that look on your face, son. I'm trying to help you find balance. That's what I always did and taught you kids. You need to find the balance between work and home, and always remember, the point of work is home, and not the other way round."

"Yes, Dad," Henry said, looking less irritated. "I do understand and am trying. I understand about the balance. I hope that Zoe will round that balance off better—"

"That's not her job, Henry." Marshall added. "I never grew up in a Christian home, so to hear and see how my new family functions is a beautiful thing, but I have to be honest Henry. The job is yours to balance home and work, as Dad says. Just because you're a single parent, doesn't mean you have more time to give to work—no matter how much you want to build a future for the boys."

Henry looked away. Everyone knew that when he did so, it meant he'd been challenged with something he hadn't really thought of before, and just needed time to ponder it.

"About this Zoe," Lisa interrupted, changing the subject. "What do we really know about her, other than the fact that she turned up everywhere Henry did?"

"It was God's will, I think, Mom." Henry said softly.

"Jeremy also turned up everywhere your sister was. Don't

forget that. People with an agenda will find a way to achieve their mission."

"What are you saying, Mom? That Zoe is like Jeremy?" Henry looked upset, which took everyone by surprise.

"No one is saying that, Dude," said Marshall. "Mom is just saying to be careful and alert. I'm sure she's one hundred percent legit, but in case she isn't, just be on the watch. At least initially."

"Yes," agreed Lisa.

"Fine," Henry acquiesced.

"Don't be like that, Big Brother," said Stacie. "We're just looking out for your well-being. I'll keep an eye on things as well."

CHAPTER 12

A New Day and a New Job

ONE

Saturday had been an eventful day for both Henry and Zoe. They did a quick walkthrough of the schedule that would begin on Monday. The day was bright and sunny, the boys wanted to go to Central Park and play. They decided to do a picnic as well.

Zoe wished them well. She told the boys to have fun and she would see them on Monday.

Jordan yelled out, "Ms. Zoe, do you want to come too? We're going to have lots of fun and we can teach you how to play the games we like the most."

Zoe was touched. She would have loved to stay but didn't want to intrude.

"Thanks Jordan. Today is your day with your dad. You guys have a good time and I will see you on Monday," Zoe replied.

Henry stepped in, "We don't mind at all. This will give us a chance to get a feel for each other and you can see the boys in action. To see what you're up against. They are some busy little rascals. On second thought, maybe you shouldn't see them. They might scare you away."

"I've had a fair share of young boys under my care. I haven't found one that has outrun me yet," Zoe laughed.

"Be careful what you ask for. My boys are super active. We would be more than honored for you to hang out with us. There is a deli up the street. We can grab some food for our picnic, Henry replied.

Just then Henry's cell rang. It was Stacie asking where they were. She decided to join them for their picnic. She offered to pick up lunch so that they would have more time to play with the boys.

Junior yelled, "I want to play tag."

Jordan stated, "Tag is for boys. We have to find a game a girl can play."

At that moment, Zoe ran pass Jordan and tapped him on the shoulder.

"Hey Jordan, you're it." Zoe screamed.

Junior and Henry were laughing so hard, they couldn't stand up straight.

Henry teased Jordan, "Son, you should never underestimate the skills of a beautiful woman."

They played tag for a little while longer and Henry bought kites from a vendor in the park.

Zoe was having the time of her life. She was running and looking at her kite soar when she lost her balance. She ran right into the back of Henry, who was running in the opposite direction, and they both tumbled to the ground.

"We have to stop meeting like this Zoe," Henry chuckled.

Henry helped Zoe up and they were standing face to face. Neither spoke for a moment as they gazed into each other's eyes. They both were rendered speechless for what seemed like eternity.

"Hey dad, Aunt Stacie is here and we're hungry," Junior announced.

Henry and Zoe turned around to see the boys seated on the blanket while Stacie stood with a knowing smile on her face. The pair joined the others for a delicious lunch.

After the boys were done eating, they ran off to play on the swings. There was an awkward silence between Henry and Zoe. They both didn't know how to process the moment they both shared.

"Zoe, what do you like to do in your spare time," Stacie asked. "Now that Jessica's married and about to be a mom, she is too busy to hang out when I come to town. I have no one to have any girl time with anymore. I love my brother but he can be quite dull and doesn't know anything about the latest styles."

"Hey, I'm right here or did you forget," Henry inquired.

Stacie laughed," You're a workaholic and you can't tell me the difference between a pump and a stiletto."

"Ha," said Henry. "I'm not that clueless. They're both purses.

Stacie and Zoe both looked at Henry and laughed.

"Zoe, like I was saying before we were so rudely interrupted by this fashion genius, let's get together sometime. I'm here for a few more days and I'm dying to do something fun.

Zoe accepted Stacie's offer.

TWO

Zoe slept the morning away. Classes were extremely busy this week. Saturday after leaving the Stones, she taught two classes. She was tired and her feet and back ached, but she'd gotten full classes and even a few customer praises. Tony was thrilled until the evening ended and she resigned. He was sad to see her go, but also happy about the opportunity she'd been given.

When she eventually woke up Sunday, she made herself lunch, as Emma and Bets were at the hospital. She suspected that Emma probably knew by now about her resignation, as she was sure that Gina would have told her. She knew that Emma would mellow out if given a chance to relax at home, and so Zoe headed to the evening service at Christ the Redeemer Church. Emma would arrive home around the time the service began, and that should be time enough for her chill.

By the time she arrived home after the service, Emma had been relaxing a good two hours already in her room. Bets had gone out for the evening with her boyfriend. Their conversation—thankfully it was a conversation and not a confrontation—had been civil and cordial enough. Emma was annoyed that, after helping her get the job, she'd resigned so fast, especially after her long speech about never again doing nanny work. She gave the same explanation which she'd given Henry, which Emma accepted but not as convincingly as Henry had. She chalked it down to Henry being a Christian and understanding about providence and God's will, and Emma not being a Christian.

That night, as Zoe lay in bed, she felt at peace. She would be fulfilling her promise to God and herself in helping the Stones, and she was still on good terms with her best friend. All was well in her life and she fell asleep with little trouble.

THREE

As Henry and the boys slept the night away, Stacie lay awake until late in the night wondering what to do about Zoe. She was a sweet, caring, warm and gentle soul, that much was clear. But Stacie knew that getting Henry open to the idea of falling in love again was going to be a hard sale. She knew that

Judith would want Henry to move on with his life and find someone that would once again complete her family.

FOUR

When Zoe arrived in the apartment at 6:30 AM on Monday morning, it was obvious that everyone was fast asleep. What surprised her was the sound of loud snoring coming from the upstairs bedrooms. Heading up the stairs quietly, she realized that the sound was coming from the guest bedroom. Sighing with relief and smiling happily knowing it was Stacie, immediately caused her to pause.

Why on Earth should I be relieved that it's Stacie and not Henry snoring so loudly? she asked herself, shaking her head and heading back downstairs to the kitchen.

In the kitchen, she started frying eggs, bacon, making toast, and then brewing fresh coffee. At seven exactly, an alarm rang upstairs, and then she heard Henry moving around in his room and in the en suite.

She headed upstairs to wake the boys, who were still fast asleep. Jordan was the easiest to wake up and get him into the bathroom to freshen up and start dressing. Junior was a different story. But being older, she felt it good to establish trust, and so told him to get up and get done, while she helped Jordan and checked on breakfast. She would then give him the freedom to get done and check on him in ten minutes.

Downstairs, she set the table in the dining room for three and brought the food out, as well as coffee for Henry and juice for the boys.

Heading back upstairs, she found Jordan completely entangled in his uniform and she straightened him out. She then sent him to brush his teeth, he'd washed his face, but forgot to brush his teeth. She then took him with her to check on Junior who was still in bed.

She gently and playfully pulled him out of bed by his feet and told him that if he wasn't dressed in five minutes, she would have no other choice but to dress him herself—expecting him not to be happy with her seeing him in a state of undress—which he frowned at and immediately started dressing. She reminded him to brush his teeth and then gave him an important task that would also ensure he was done, downstairs, and on time.

She asked him to check on his father and bring him down with him when he was ready to come downstairs. The smile on his face at his task, made her smile as well, knowing that she would not need to come back upstairs to check on him. Ten minutes later, Henry and Junior entered the dining room, both were dressed and freshened up. Jordan was already eating.

"Well, this definitely works!" Henry said, smiling happily at the table with two dressed boys. "Breakfast looks delicious!" He said, sitting down and dishing for himself. He tasted the coffee he poured for himself. "Oh my! Zoe, this is amazing!" He said, smacking his lips.

Zoe blushed and took a seat next to Jordan, who was trying to cram all his bacon into his mouth in one go.

"Slow down, kiddo," she said, pulling some of the bacon out of his mouth.

Junior looked completely grossed out by both his brother and Zoe's fingers pulling pieces of bacon from his mouth.

"This is so crispy," said Henry. "It's just like Mom used to make, remember, buddy?" He asked Junior. For a moment, Junior just stared at his father and then looked at Zoe. When she glanced at Junior and their eyes locked, in that split second, she could have sworn she saw scorn in them.

Junior looked away quickly. A minute earlier he'd been digging into breakfast without gusto. And now he dropped his fork onto the plate and focused on his juice.

"What time do you need to be at work today?" She asked Henry.

And so they launched into a discussion about his work and some of the issues he had to sort out that day at the office.

Once they finished, she sent the boys upstairs to get their school bags and be ready to leave. Henry also fetched his brief-case, while she cleared the table.

When all three came downstairs again, a visitor had arrived. It was Carol. This time, she simply entered the apart-ment without first buzzing to be let in. She was leaving to take Rebecca in early and would give Henry and the boys a lift.

"That's so sweet," said Henry. "I think we'll pass, though. Zoe needs to get used to the routine and also see where the school is and what the morning traffic is like."

"Oh, hello Zoe," Carol said with a wide shark-like smile that was all teeth. "I almost didn't see you there, dear. Don't you look lovely? I think I should come over later and show you some tips for your hair that will absolutely make you look pretty."

They all stood ready to leave in the lift foyer.

"Thank you, but I have other plans once I drop the boys off," said Zoe, taking the barb in stride.

"I used to be a hair stylist back in the day. I'm sure I can fix your hair to look like something nice, especially with your skin being so dark," Carol continued.

"No thank you," Zoe said again. Zoe couldn't do anything but stare. She didn't know what kind of relationship Carol had with Henry, but she was not one to be a doormat. She took pride in who she was but before she was anything else, she was a child of God and made in his image. Zoe decided to turn the other cheek, but she would definitely have a conversa-tion with Henry.

Henry looked very uncomfortable between the two women. Junior, however, looked from Zoe to Carol, and as he and Carol locked eyes, an understanding seemed to pass between them.

"Anyway," said Carol, looking at Henry. "Nonsense about all that. She can use Google to get them this afternoon. You do know how to find locations with Google, don't you?" She turned back to Zoe.

"Yes," replied Zoe.

"There we go. Besides, with such a big change in their routine, it'll be nice to have some familiarity again." She looked at Junior. "What do you say, young man? Want to travel with Aunt Carol again?"

Junior looked at Zoe, and with a smirk, said, "Sure, that'd be really great, Aunt Carol." He said this without taking his eyes off Zoe.

"And it's settled. Zoe, you stay and get cleaning, while I drop the boys off with my daughter."

"Just the dishes from breakfast is fine," Henry told Zoe.

"Oh, nonsense, she's a worker after all. They clean everything. The place could use a good vacuum and dusting. And a wash too," said Carol.

"Goodness Carol, she's not the maid, she's the nanny. She works every day," corrected Henry, moving past the women to press the lift button.

"Aah, apologies Zoe," said Carol while Henry's back was turned. "I just..." she paused and fixed a scornful glare at her, "... assumed." Carol turned to face the lift doors, as they opened.

"Well Carol, I think you need to keep your assumptions to yourself," Henry scornfully said.

"Zoe, the dishes will be fine. The cleaning service will take care of the rest. Enjoy your day. If you need anything, give me a call," Henry stated.

Henry and the boys followed Carol into the lift. Henry smiled nervously at Zoe, who smiled back and greeted the boys. Jordan waved back enthusiastically while Junior looked to his side as the doors closed.

FIVE

After dropping Henry off at work, Carol dropped Rebecca off at school. Before Henry was dropped off, he noted how furious Rebecca seemed to be about being up so early. When Jordan hopped out at their school, Carol asked to have a word with Junior.

"She seems so nice, don't you think?" She asked.

"Zoe? I guess," said Junior.

"So motherly. It's just what you, Jordan, and Daddy need. A new mommy. You must be so happy."

"A new mommy?" Junior asked, puzzled. He looked at Carol with large eyes.

"Why yes, to take your old mommy's place. Jordan and Daddy seem so happy to have her. You should be happy too."

"We don't need a new mommy," he replied softly. "We have a mommy. We're just fine as we are. Aren't we?"

"Well, it's not really up to me. It's up to you to choose for yourself."

"It is?"

"Of course. Dad would hate to see you unhappy. If he saw you and Zoe not getting along, and if you were unhappy all the time, he'd definitely have to let her go."

"Oh," replied Junior, as the thought and its implications settled in his mind.

CHAPTER 13

A Crisis on All Fronts

ONE

Henry was busy putting the finishing touches to the Robert Morgan file when Stacie visited him at the office. She would have been in his office ten minutes earlier already, but Hannah had been so excited to see her and talk to her that Stacie felt like she'd been taken hostage. Hannah hadn't seen Stacie nor William in years. When she eventually managed to free herself from Hannah, she dropped into the couch in Henry's office.

"Honestly, is that how all my interviewees feel?" She wheezed, breathing heavily.

"What do you mean?" asked Henry, laughing.

"I swear Hannah now knows my bra size! That's how exhaustively I was interrogated," she laughed. "I was asked every single question you can think of as well as the hundred others you wouldn't ever have thought of!"

"She's just excited to see you, sis. When was the last time you saw her? Three years ago?"

"But still, dude!" Stacie held her head, as though it were a motion-sensitive bomb. "It's not my fault she's stuck having to look at your sorry mug every day! All I wanted to do was pop in to see how things went this morning, to see how you are, and I literally got the third degree as though I was caught sneaking out of the house!"

"I think you're being punished," Henry said, trying to sound full of sagely wisdom.

"Oh, *really*? And for what?"

"For being horrible to your dear older brother."

"Listen, 'dear older brother,' someone's got to keep you on your feet, or otherwise, look at all of this nonsense you get yourself into!" Henry went and sat on the couch opposite her.

"So, what have I done now to warrant a work visit?"

"Nothing, silly. As I said, I just wanted to check in on you, personally. Now that we have Zoe at home, that lightens your load with the boys. And you did promise that with the Morgan case resolved you would be working normal hours again. So I want to see how you're coping."

"With what? All is sorted."

"But is it, really? It's been a hard road since Judith passed. You were immediately thrown into the deep end caring for the boys and helping them through their loss. Jordan was still a toddler basically and needed your full attention all the time."

"Yes! It has been a rough journey" she sighed. "Continuing, we then had to deal with Jessica being stalked and terrorized by that scumbag, Jeremy. And just when we thought things would start going swimmingly again, Dad had his stroke last year. And then the twisting of the knife, Robert Morgan."

Henry sat back stunned. *Had so much happened in such a short space?* He wondered. And how could I have forgotten so much of it? Okay, that's not entirely correct. I haven't forgotten, I've just not thought much about it.

"Henry? Are you still with me?"

"Yes, I was just... thinking."

"It's a lot to take in, yes. And through one crisis after the next you've not had anyone take care of you."

"I'm okay though. I am. I have to be for the boys."

"Yes, you have to be for them, but that doesn't happen automatically. Have you ever really spoken to someone about all of this, Henry?"

"Like a psychiatrist you mean?"

"Or your pastor."

"I read my Bible and say my prayers. God has helped me through all these tough times."

"And I love that about you, I do. You inspire me when I feel like throwing the towel in, but trust me when I tell you, you have all of God's resources available to you, not just prayer and the Bible, as powerful as those are. You have the Church, you have your pastor, you have your family, so make use of all of the tools God has given. Speak to me, speak to Dad or Will. Or if not us, which is cool, then take my advice and speak to your pastor."

"I promise, I'll think and pray on it. If it is God's will, then who am I to resist? I just feel that bad things happen for a reason, to make us stronger. And that's what's happened."

"No, don't do that. Remember what Dad used to tell us as kids, never try to be as smart as Job's friends. You will only get it all wrong. The only truth to bad times is that God is in control of the bad times as well as the good. He's with you through it all, always."

"I know."

"Okay. So how did the first day go with Zoe? Sorry, I was out like a light. I woke up late and the house was spotless. She was out. Fetching the boys, I assume."

"Yeah, Carol is to thank for that. She came around this morning and collected me and the boys—"

"What do you mean? Zoe was supposed to do that to see where the school was." She said angrily.

"Well, Carol has a mind of her own. She told her to clean the house as well."

"Henry! How can you allow her to tell Zoe what to do! That's not okay!" Stacie was livid. Henry had rarely seen her this worked up in a long time. "You need to step up here, dude, and protect your nanny. And put that woman in her place!"

"Stacie, don't worry about it. I got it under control. I didn't have the time this morning but it will be handled." Henry said sharply. He didn't tolerate bullying of any kind, regardless of who it was.

"Oh, have I annoyed you?" Stacie goaded.

Stacie leaned in closer, "Oh, really? Then why allow Carol to do precisely that to Zoe, and in front of you, doing nothing!"

Henry felt like a hammer had just been driven into his midsection.

"You let her demean and belittle her like that!"

He realized that he'd walked right into that fatal blow. He'd always hated arguing with Stacie. Everyone had always said when they were kids that Stacie was going to be a lawyer because no one ever won an argument against her.

He sat back in his seat, ashamed of himself.

Stacie could see that Henry had genuinely not thought of Carol as a bully in terms of how she'd treated Zoe but did now. "Just please make sure you put Carol in her place. Zoe should be allowed to do her job, without that woman's shadow over her all the time."

"Okay," he said softly.

"Has she spoken again about her family? Her mother?"

"Who?" asked Henry, narrowing his eyes at his sister. *What now?* he thought to himself.

"Zoe. Has she said anything more about her mother, for example?"

"No. Why? What's going on? What's going through your mind?"

"Nothing, I was just wondering, is all. If she had."

"Stacie?" He knew better than to ignore his sister's intuition. And she never spoke a word without intention.

"What? I'm just curious about her family and her story, especially seeing as how she grew up around the corner from us basically."

Henry stared at her, uneasily, and he could see she noticed.

"Honestly, I am curious, it's a small world," she said. "Stop seeing devils behind everything I ask."

He looked at her and she smiled to reassure him that all was well. He smiled back, relieved.

One less worry to have, he thought to himself.

TWO

As Stacie walked out of the Bremicker Building, she thought about the last words that she and Henry had exchanged, it had gotten her thinking about Zoe. *Seeing as how we grew up around the corner from each other basically. That was, somehow, the key*, she thought to herself as she got into her Uber.

THREE

When Zoe arrived at the school, she was early and so waited almost 30 minutes for the siren to sound. After the siren sounded, she waited another 20 minutes until all the kids had come through the gate and most had been collected, leaving only a few stragglers still waiting for their lifts.

Sighing, she entered the school and spoke to one of the staff. She was happy to know that Henry had indeed notified the school that she would be collecting the boys, and he'd provided her details for reference. After another 15 minutes of checking the school premises and inquiring with the class teachers, it was confirmed that the boys were no longer on the premises.

Zoe was about to make a panicked call to Henry, when a teacher ran up to them, and informed her that the blonde woman who normally picks them up had fetched them directly from their classes when the siren went off.

"I'm so sorry, I was unaware of the new change. Was I not supposed to let them go with her?" She asked Zoe in concern, who could only wipe away her tears of stress and shrug her shoulders.

FOUR

Henry was about to leave the office to hand-deliver his file on Robert Morgan to the police when Hannah raced into his office. She was beyond anxious and flustered.

"What is it?" He asked, seeing how distressed she was.

"Lawrence says we've been hacked, Mister Stone!" She shouted in a panic.

"Hacked? What do you mean? How?"

Lawrence then came into the office as well—he was the same age as Henry, just far rounder and heavier.

"Mister Stone, our firewall has been breached and confidential customer data has been downloaded off the server," said Lawrence, out of breath from having raced from the other end of the floor to Henry's office.

"What!" Henry shouted. "How much? Whose data? Was it specific customers?" He rattled off questions.

"No, it was everything. They downloaded everything and as far as I can tell, uploaded a virus, and corrupted all of the original files. It's all gone, Henry!" The other man shouted.

FIVE

When Zoe eventually arrived home, the apartment was empty. Breathing heavily and beyond frustrated, she sat on the couch and said a prayer to calm herself and refocus her mind. She then entered the lift and selected the apartment below theirs. After waiting five minutes in the lift, Carol answered laughing.

"Yes, Carol here. Is that you Zena?"

"It's Zoe here, not Zena. Are the boys with you?"

"Yes, of course, I'd never leave them unattended at school."

"Can you please send them out?" She asked courteously.

"No, it's fine. My Rebecca is helping them with their homework. I've just made dinner as well, so we'll have a bite, and then when Henry arrives, he can collect them. You can probably head home if you're done for the day. Ta-ta!"

The elevator made another beeping sound, which Zoe took to mean Carol had terminated the call.

Uncertain whether she could still be seen in the lift, and not wanting to cause any offense, she maintained self-control and pressed the button for the Stone apartment.

Henry was meant to be home by five that day, but by 5:15, he'd still not arrived. Fifteen minutes later he called and apologized for being late, they had developed another major crisis at work and he had to tend to it.

When he asked how the boys were, she explained the situation, but could tell that Henry wasn't really listening. He asked her to refer any issues with the boys to Stacie. She then explained that Stacie had not returned home since leaving before lunch. He then asked if she could stay later to mind the boys until he got home, and he would take her home.

She felt it a waste to explain that the boys were not in her care presently, and so quietly agreed. She never saw Stacie at all that evening, but Henry arrived home just after nine.

The boys were dropped off by Rebecca at 7:30. Zoe got them showered and dressed for bed. Bringing Jordan to Junior's bed, she read to them from a children's fantasy novel. Jordan seemed to love the story and was especially impressed with the different voices Zoe put on for the different characters. He also adored the sound effects she made while reading to them. Junior, seemed completely unimpressed or interested.

After 30 minutes, she sent Jordan to his own room and switched their lights off.

CHAPTER 14

The Plot Thickens

ONE

When Zoe entered the lounge, she found Henry sitting on the couch, leaning forward with his head in his hands, looking at the floor. She could feel the stress and tension emanating from him. She wished she could help him somehow—it was why she was here after all—however, it was already late, and she needed to get home. The boys were fast asleep. He had said nothing about the Carol situation, but given how stressed he was, she felt it better to fight that battle another day.

"Henry?" She asked softly.

"Don't you wish sometimes you could just rewind and restart your day? To just erase everything that went wrong and start over?"

"My mother always used to say that if wishes were kisses, we'd all have lovers," she replied with a weak smile. "I never really got my mom sometimes, she had these weird sayings."

"My dad has so many weird sayings, but they always

taught you something, if you wanted to learn. I think your mom meant that if people always got what they wanted, then they'd always get the girl or guy they wanted. No more broken hearts."

"Yeah, I get that, but what about the girl or guy who didn't want to be '*got*' by you? Or they wanted to be 'got' by someone else? She used to say that to me when I moaned about nursing school. She would tell me that we don't always get what we want, and then throw in that line."

"And then it was over." Henry chuckled.

"Oh, you knew it was over," she laughed. "Moms can end arguments like no one else can!"

Henry smiled, sighed, and then looked grave again.

"I'm very sorry about today. I know things have gone all wrong. I'll find some way to deal with everything tomorrow. I just have... far too much on top of me now. I thought having you here would make things easier, but things are anything but." Looking at Zoe, he saw her face drop. "Not your fault, and not in any way regretting taking you on. I just mean, I thought everything was on the way upwards, but things with Carol are not going upward and things at work... well," he sighed, pausing, "... things are speeding downhill at work."

Zoe looked towards the lift foyer, down at her backpack, and then looked at Henry. She nodded to herself and took a seat on the couch facing him.

"Can you tell me what happened at work, please?" She asked him.

"I really shouldn't—" He started.

"Please?" She asked and smiled. "You asked me on Saturday to say what I saw, to be open with you. Well, now you can be open with me."

"A man called Robert Morgan became so angry that another staff member, Rachel, won a work prize that he hacked into her cloud and shared explicit photos of her with all the staff. We fired him basically—fully compliant and legally, mind you—and thought that was the end of it. We were going to hand over all our findings and files to the police, as it's now a civil and legal issue... we were doing that today."

"But that wasn't the end of it," said Zoe.

"No, not even close," sighed Henry. *You sigh too often lately for your own good,* he thought to himself. "Robert then hacked 2-b-frank's database, erased all our files, and copied them for himself. All our customer details are now in his hands."

"Oh, Henry," Zoe said, feeling his distress. "I'm so sorry."

"Oh, it gets better. Seems Robert then sent a threatening email to Rachel, telling her that he has even more explicit material of her and that he will release it publicly."

"But why? For what purpose?"

"Rachel is instituting civil proceedings against him. He threatened to release the material unless she withdraws the suit. He also sent her a screenshot of a police identity file of one, Robert Williams, who had been arrested ten years prior for cybercrimes."

"Oh no! Are they the same person?"

"Both Rachel and I are having our legal representatives look into it, so I can't confirm or deny yet, but it seems to be the case."

"He changed his name?"

"It would seem so."

"Wait," said Zoe, as a thought occurred to her. "What about you? Did you get an email as well?"

"Indeed," said Henry.

"What does he want from you?"

"For us to destroy all evidence of his crimes and in exchange, we get our files back."

"So you can't hand over the report to the police, basically. What will you do?"

"I don't know. He could ruin the company my father built with the data he has. And to top it, Rachel doesn't want to back down. She's more determined than ever. In fact, she feels so strongly that her lawyer advised us that they are considering a suit against us, as well."

"For what?" She asked.

"For not providing a secure environment for her and the rest of the staff, for not properly vetting Robert and picking up his false ID. It was just a long list the lawyer shared earlier. Nothing formal yet."

They sat in silence, staring past one another. "What will you do, Henry?"

"I really don't know. I'm not even supposed to talk to anyone about this, confidentiality and all. I can't tell my dad, and yet I've told you. I don't know."

"Thank you for trusting me with this. I won't speak of it to anyone." She paused and watched his facial expressions. "What do you *think* you should do? What's the right thing to do?"

"I don't know!" He groaned and brought his fist onto the arm of the couch. "I wish I knew. I should protect my staff, Stacie said as much earlier today. Defend those who are being bullied, and Robert Morgan, or Williams, is a bully for sure. But how do I do that? Do I let him get away with this?"

"Can I be frank with you again, like I was about Carol?"

"Yes."

"This man has committed crimes against Rachel, you, the company, and the staff. To not hand over the files, is to allow him to continue those crimes, and get away with it. Don't do that. Don't let him get away. Find a way to bring him to justice and protect your staff and your dad's company."

"On paper, that's easy and sounds possible, but in real life... it's a different situation."

"Not really, right is right and wrong is wrong. Bullies need to be stopped. And protecting your company and all within the company is how you do that."

"I know all of that. That's all I have been thinking about. If I make the files disappear, there's no stopping him from destroying the data he stole or using it against us for some other evil scheme."

"Exactly."

"But the minute I hand the files over, he'll sink us."

"And that's what you should be focusing on preventing. You clearly know what you need to do, now you need the strength to do it, and you need to find a way to get those files back. For your sake, the companies, and Rachel's."

Henry looked away. *That really was the gist of it, the crux of the matter,* he thought. *She is right. I know what I need to do, I just need the strength to do it. And a plan to prevent Robert from carrying out his threat.*

"Henry?"

"Sorry," he said, looking into her eyes, and getting lost in them. He shook his head quickly, to clear his mind. "What about Rachel? How do I get her to not come after the company then?"

"Have you actually tried talking to her about this? How did you deal with her during this situation?"

"Well, we arranged counseling to help her—"

"But did you speak to her and try to offer her your counsel and your comfort?"

"I don't think it would be appropriate for me to try to 'comfort' her after her ordeal."

"But you're thinking not as a Christian, but as a man of the world. 'Comfort' doesn't mean sitting down and hugging her. It means offering your sympathies, telling her you're there for her, and that you're sorry, that you will do whatever you can to see that she finds justice. Did you make her realize that she's not alone and while she is free to pursue her own civil case with her own lawyer, you will be with her every step of the way? Did you tell her she can make use of your lawyer?"

"That's not how the world works, Zoe. It sounds sweet and fantastic, but the real world has rules and regulations about—"

"God's Word supersedes those rules and regulations. It's for you to offer, and her to accept or decline. But then it means you have done right by her in God's eyes and your own eyes. And even if she declines, she will never forget what you offered, and how you exposed yourself *for her*."

Henry looked away again and sat back.

She was beginning to understand that this was his way of processing things. "Well bossman, it seems like my ride needs to come, it is getting late."

Henry giggled. "Bossman? Seriously?" She enjoyed seeing him smiling and laughing.

"Well, you pay the checks, bossman."

"Get outta here, kid," said Henry, waving her away, but laughing. "I'll send for an Uber. I feel awful I can't take you home, but I thought Stacie—"

"Relax, bossman. It's all good," said Zoe, smiling. "The kids are asleep, so you have no choice. Uber is fine." She stood up. "I'll just pop into the ladies room while you arrange the Uber." She turned towards the downstairs toilet.

"Zoe," said Henry. She stopped and looked at him. "Thank you. Your words were like a light in a very dark place. You have no idea how blessed I feel to have you in the family."

She smiled warmly. "Thank you, Henry, it's my pleasure."

"No more 'bossman' then? I was just getting used to it. I was going to add it to our contract."

"Oh hush you!" Zoe replied, without thinking. As the

words left her mouth, a pang of regret and fear prodded her tummy. Henry, however, laughed and smiled at her with such adoration in his eyes, that she returned the smile, knowing all was well.

Fifteen minutes later, she was in the Uber and on the way home for the night.

TWO

It was just after ten when Stacie came home. She was exhausted as she had a busy day tending to some banking issues that needed her attention. She'd also popped into the Nuri Spa for a full body massage and then treated herself to a late dinner. In between these activities, she'd also spent time researching Zoe James. Her research had thus far uncovered very little.

When she headed upstairs to her room, she heard the shower running in Henry's bathroom, and so waited in her room until he'd finished. When she was sure he was done, she popped in to greet.

They chatted for a bit about unimportant things. She didn't want to harp on the Carol situation, but she hoped that he would tell her that he'd spoken to her. Saying nothing about Carol, she guessed that he'd not done so yet. She asked him if there was any other news from the day, and he said no, and with that, they both went to bed.

THREE

Henry didn't discuss the newest developments at work with Stacie, as he wanted to try to figure things out for himself first. Zoe's advice and concern had touched him greatly and gotten him thinking. He wanted to do the right thing, and she'd helped him to identify what the right thing was in this instant.

Once he had a better idea of how to implement that though, he would speak with her about what was happening. The other concern he had was Dad finding out and getting stressed. He agreed it was bad to keep secrets, but he also felt it was equally bad to share devastating news without having some sort of possible solution to share as well.

CHAPTER 15
Trial by Fire

ONE

Stacie looked at the kitchen clock. It was almost 7:30 AM already and Zoe had still not arrived for work. She was meant to be in by 6:30. Henry had to leave early at six to attend to some issue, which frustrated her to no end knowing he was keeping something from her. She'd gotten the boys up, dressed, and fed already when she saw Zoe was late.

She didn't want to add to her brother's stress by contacting him to ask where she was, so she sat in the kitchen, staring at the clock. She wasn't sure if she should be worried that something bad had happened to Zoe, or if she was just delayed, or if she'd resigned. The problem was that without contacting Henry, she had no way to reach Zoe as she didn't have her phone number.

The lift beeped and she sighed with relief. When she opened the lift and saw Carol and Rebecca, she sighed again, but this time in annoyance. Carol was leaving to drop Rebecca, and asked if she could drop the boys as well.

"No, it's fine, I'm about to leave anyway to drop them off," she said.

"Oh?" Carol frowned, looking around the apartment. "Where's Zelda?"

"Zoe, and she's running late."

"And it's only the second day. I'll have to have a word with Henry. Not good at all. She looks the type, mind you," said Carol.

"What type is that?"

"The type to take advantage of a naïve man's good heart. For a nanny, it's highly unprofessional to be late. It throws the whole day off for Henry."

"Henry is fine, I'll take the boys to school, no problem."

"Oh, that's fine, I'm going that way, anyway," insisted Carol.

Stacie looked at her. "Sure. As for Henry, I'll be speaking to him about Zoe, so no need to concern yourself there." She held Carol's gaze, who stared back.

"Of course," said Carol.

"Boys!" Stacie shouted.

Jordan and Junior came out of the lounge with their bags, ready to leave. Junior and Carol exchanged smiles as they entered the lift.

TWO

Just before nine, the doors to the lift opened and Zoe entered the apartment. She was flustered and frustrated. Stacie came immediately to her.

"Where have you been?" She asked, her tone a mixture of concern and frustration of her own.

"Did Henry not call you yet?" Zoe asked, out of breath.

"No, why would he?"

"He had to override the elevator security. Somehow the

elevator was set to *Night Security Mode*, or something like that."

"*Night Security*?" asked Stacie, bewildered. The concept rang a bell. The elevator could be programmed to not allow access to the apartment between certain hours, neither via the doors opening on the floor, nor via beeping in the lift foyer or ringing the primary cell phone—Henry's phone. It meant that if the hours were set from 10 PM to 6 AM then only authorized people like Henry and Stacie could enter or exit the apartment via the lift. Visitors or other tenants couldn't, nor could they even beep Henry or the lift foyer. It was to ensure the apartment was 'locked' for the night. It also prevented accidental beeping during the night by a visitor of another tenant.

"*Night Security* is only on at night, it deactivates at six," said Stacie.

"Yes, but apparently not. It was still on, Henry had to deactivate it. I've been trying to get in since just after six."

"Really?" Stacie asked.

"Yes, Henry told me he's leaving very early, so I tried to get in earlier, but I was stuck on the lift. Eventually after almost 30 minutes, I went back down to Walter, and after checking, he said the *Night Security* must have glitched and remained active."

"That's... odd."

"He said only Henry could deactivate it, but we couldn't reach him. Eventually I searched for 2-b-frank on the internet and found the office number, called, and spoke to Henry."

"And here you are."

"Yes," sighed Zoe. She could see that Stacie was doubting her story.

"Take a break and lie down on the couch. I'll make you some coffee, if you would like."

Zoe put her bag down in the dining room and turned back

to Stacie. "I'd rather get started with lunch. I assume that you took the boys to school?"

"No, Carol took them."

"I see," Zoe said, unable to hide her disappointment. "How did she get into the apartment, though?" She asked, frowning.

"She has access. During *Night Security Mode*, anyone with access can still get in and out using the lift." Stacie went to the kitchen and scratched through one of the drawers. "I saw this stupid booklet in here the other day when I was looking for the recipe book that came with the air fryer. Here we go!" She pulled out a small booklet and handed it to Zoe. The cover read, *'Kensington security and elevator features.'* "Have a read through about it all."

THREE

Zoe put a lasagna in the oven, and then looked at the booklet about the lifts. She noticed a specific set of instructions and then walked to the lift foyer with the booklet. She found the control panel, and lifted the cover, exposing the display and keypad.

Punching in the necessary codes and instructions, she checked whose code had been entered when the *Night Security* feature had last been programmed. Finding the five-digit code, she then accessed the code legend and cross-referenced the codes. There were quite a few people with assigned codes, besides her and Carol. All of Henry's family had codes as well. But the code that had been used to change the Night Security settings belonged to only one person. She sighed when she saw the name.

❧

Zoe arrived at the boy's school earlier than the day before. This time she went to wait by the pedestrian gate—the gate the kids exited from, to ensure the boys were not smuggled past her again.

Junior was the first to come out. As he emerged, he was happy and laughing with his classmates, but when he saw her, he looked surprised and his mood changed visibly.

"You're here?" He asked, looking surprised.

"Of course. Why wouldn't I be?" she asked. "I have to fetch you and drop you at school every day. Daddy depends on me for that."

"Oh. I thought you might have left," he said and pushed past her. He saw the car and started walking towards it.

Zoe saw Jordan running towards her from inside the gate. She turned to Junior and saw he was walking on. "Junior, just wait for Jordan with me please."

Ignoring her, he continued walking towards the car.

"Junior! Stop please, and come back here," she said louder. Jordan grabbed and hugged her as he came through the gate. "Junior!" She squeezed Jordan, but still shouted after Junior.

He continued ignoring her. Looking around, Zoe was concerned that a car might hit him, driving through the lot. She saw a car reversing out of a bay, very near him. "Junior!" she screamed loudly, startling him.

And then Carol was there, grabbing him into her arms, and lifting him off the ground. She carried him towards Zoe.

"Goodness, whatever is the matter with you? Are you crazy?" She shouted at Zoe. "The poor boy could have been killed!"

"Zoe?"

"Carol, thank you for collecting Junior. I'll—"

"I am Miss Gillespie to you, and please hand over that child now." She pointed to Jordan. "You're not fit to mind these boys! This poor child was almost killed!"

"I'm grateful for your help. I'm sorry for..." She paused, a tear running down her cheek. "I'm sorry about that, I was trying to get him to come back to me."

"Oh, so it's his fault? He's a child, you fool!" screamed Carol, making a scene. "Don't you have children of your own? Do you know nothing about looking after children?"

Zoe looked around, everyone was staring at them. The teachers from the day before were coming closer to defuse the situation. "If you feel that I have done something wrong, then you're welcome to address that with Henry. However, do not speak to me in such a way."

"Mister Stone, not 'Henry!' Mister Stone. The disrespect and contempt you have—"

"Enough!" said Zoe, sternly and loudly. She saw Junior even flinched. "Do not speak to me as though I am some child. I do not work for you, I work for Henry. He has hired me and until he dismisses me, I'll continue to do my job. Junior, come here now please, to your brother, and then we will be going to the car. **Now**!"

Carol smiled. "It's fine Junior. Go with her. I'll drive behind you to make sure she doesn't put you in any more danger. Then I'll talk to your daddy and get rid of this woman."

Zoe held her hand out to Junior, who reluctantly came to her. "Remember boys, that a bully is someone who tries to hurt you with bad words, but at the end of the day, a bully is just a small person with a bad attitude who thinks so little of themselves that they think little of everyone else as well."

Carol's mouth almost hit the floor in stunned shock.

FOUR

Henry sat in the boardroom with Rachel Lee and her lawyer, Wilson Jones. Rachel was an attractive and petite Asian-American woman with short black hair in a pixie cut. It had been almost three weeks since he'd last seen her. His solution to her claims against Robert was to put her on paid sick leave; it had come from a good place, though. But after speaking with Zoe, he realized more should have been done and so he'd requested an urgent meeting with them.

He started the meeting by apologizing to her for the way he'd handled the whole situation. He explained that while he was without excuse, this was nonetheless a new situation to him. He wanted to do better and he wanted the opportunity to make things right. He understood that offering her therapy might have been good and necessary for her, but it had also been cowardly of him, and dismissive. And so, he assured her that he was available to her any time, whether for updates on the case, or just to get things off her chest, or for anything work related. He understood her fear of Robert and her anger at being vulnerable at the office. He promised they would do all that they could to ensure all staff were safe in future.

As for Robert, they would actively try to thwart all his plans to extort both her and 2-b-frank.

When Wilson asked how protecting the staff in future would help his client, Henry told him that Rachel would always be staff, regardless of whether she continued suing the company or not. She would always have a place at 2-b-frank. She was one of their top designers and much of the company's success in the last five years was due to her.

Rachel and Wilson then requested time to process all that had been said and promised and agreed to a follow up meeting on Friday. Henry assured them that he would have some sort of plan to share with them by Friday, to deal with Robert.

CHAPTER 16

The Patience of Job

ONE

When Henry arrived at home, he felt great. He felt as though something momentous had happened in his life, as though a new chapter had begun in the story of Henry Stone. He knew that he still had an almost insurmountable challenge to overcome in Robert Morgan, or Williams.

And he knew he had to still deal with Carol. But somehow, putting himself in Rachel's shoes and sympathizing with her had rejuvenated some part of his soul. He felt like he'd done something good for the first time in a very long time—he'd made a difference in someone's life. And so when he arrived home, he was feeling ecstatic.

Carol must have been patrolling her balcony however, because the minute he entered the parking basement and made his way to the lifts, she was waiting inside. And all the way to the top floor, she detailed the many offenses Zoe had been guilty of, from her disrespectful tone and attitude, to her losing her temper, to her almost getting Junior killed, and more. And of course, Carol added her own perverse embellishments to the tales.

"Honestly Henry, that woman should not be allowed back into your apartment. It's not my place to tell you what to do, but I believe that you know what is best for your boys, as you yourself told me the other day," Carol said.

"Thank you, Carol, and you are 100% correct, it is not your place to advise me what to do when it comes to my boys. I'll deal with it, rest assured," said Henry.

TWO

Stacie was a world-famous journalist known for sniffing out the truth. Something in the back of her mind whispered that Stacie had been looking at her askew ever since the Saturday interview.

She suspects something, thought Zoe. *And that made things dangerous. It's too soon for the truth to come out. If it comes out now, then I'll be dismissed. But if it doesn't come from me... then what?*

Before she could think further on it, Henry entered the apartment and he looked anything but happy.

THREE

After greeting the boys and Stacie, Henry approached Zoe.

"Can you come to my study please?" The boys were sitting in the lounge watching TV with Stacie, who appeared to have not heard Henry.

Nodding, she followed him out of the lounge.

In his study, they sat facing each other on opposite sides of his desk.

"I can well imagine you must know what this is about?" He started off.

"Yes," she replied.

"There have been some concerning things that have happened today, and I'd like to know your side. I've heard Carol's," he said. "First let me say two things. One is I respect and trust you, because you have shown yourself to be kind, caring, and sweet. But I don't know you. I'm giving you the benefit of the doubt, because I feel in my gut I can trust you. And because your advice about Rachel..." He paused. He sat back in his chair. "I don't know if it'll end the way I'd like it to, but it felt really good talking with her. I was beyond thrilled coming home, I felt like I was walking on air, and then Carol got me and blasted the air out from under me."

"I'm sorry that your joy was stolen, Henry."

"Such is life, right? The true test of a person isn't what you do when things are going your way, but what you do when things go your way, and then are abruptly derailed."

"Yes."

"Now for the not-so-good part. The second thing I need to say to you is that I can't be partial. Not when my boys are involved. I have to be neutral for my boys. Fair?"

"Yes, of course."

"Then please tell me everything that you feel I should know."

And so Zoe did just that, outlining all the events of the day. She told the long story as is, with neither embellishment nor editing. She avoided the issue with the lift this morning.

When she finished, Henry was silent for a few moments. "So, you maintain that all of this is because Carol feels threatened by you and is trying to make you look bad so I can dismiss you?"

She sighed. "Yes."

"That doesn't take away from the fact that you allowed Junior to venture across the parking lot without supervision, during the school run, when people were driving through the lot, though!" He said sharply.

"No, it doesn't. That was an error on my part. I am sorry. I don't believe there is anything I could say that would excuse that lapse in my judgment." She looked down, ashamed to meet his gaze.

"No, look up, please." He waited until she lifted her head, and their eyes met again. "Try me. What I know of you—the little I do know of you—I do not believe you would have carelessly done so. So please tell me something. The truth."

"I allowed my irritation with Carol to get the better of me. She went to the boys' classrooms yesterday to fetch them, knowing I was sitting outside waiting, and—"

"What?" He asked, sounding both shocked and agitated. "She did what?"

"She went to their classrooms and collected them. I ran around the whole school, got the teachers involved. We were about to call you when one of the teachers told me what had happened."

Henry stared at her. He gripped the edges of the armrests, squeezing the spongy material.

"So, I wanted to make sure that I collected both boys and waited for them by the gate. Junior... is not entirely comfortable with me being in the house—"

"What do you mean? Why would you say that?"

"It's true. Don't be angry. I think he feels that I'm taking his mother's place in the home—"

"Excuse me? Where on Earth do you get off saying that? I mean, that's quite an opinion of yourself."

"Henry, please. I don't mean to offend you. I know how amazing your wife was, and what an amazing mother she was. I could never take her place and would never dream of it. I'm... I'm the furthest thing ever from her."

Hearing those words, cut Henry deep to the heart, and

knowing that he had prompted her to speak those words, was like a pain in his chest.

"I am sorry, that was uncalled for. I sometimes speak before thinking." He sighed. "Do you really think Junior feels that way?"

"I'm sorry, but yes. And my mistake was not realizing just how deeply affected he is by it. I thought it was minor, and maybe fanned a little by Carol. But the fact that he refused to listen and walked on against my pleas, makes me think it's far more serious than I thought."

"I see," said Henry.

"I misjudged the situation, and it put Junior in danger."

"And gave Carol all the rope she needed to hang you."

"She's only doing what she feels compelled to do because of her feelings for you."

FOUR

Zoe watched Henry carefully. He had been so angry when he thought she had put Junior in harm's way, and when she suggested that Junior felt she was taking his mother's place. Now, hearing that Carol was the real threat and instigator, he seemed calm. Disturbed, unhappy, even frustrated, but nonetheless, calm.

She wondered whether he did actually have feelings for Carol and therefore was so calm? But the more she thought about it, the more she felt not. Nor was he afraid of her. He was beholden to her. Since living at Kensington, Carol had been his go-to. She had helped and bailed him out numerous times—too many times to mention. And so he felt that awkward angst of wanting to rebuke her, but not knowing how to go against someone who had been like a rock in many ways for him to lean on. He was doing his looking to the side thing again though, and so Zoe took comfort in that.

Henry then said he would sleep on the matter and then think of how to raise the issue with Carol that would not ruin a friendship. He assured her however, that she was the nanny, and that she was to be respected by the boys and anyone else, Carol included. He wanted to call Junior in to speak to him about his attitude, and find out how serious it was, but Zoe pleaded with him to let her first try to resolve it. She insisted that for him to address it now, may in fact make things worse rather than better.

Henry then put some of the missing pieces together. "What happened this morning with the lift? How can that have happened for no apparent reason?"

She tried to think of something to say but floundered and Henry detected that.

"What? Did someone tamper with the settings?" He asked. She looked away. "Someone did, didn't they? Was it Carol?" He stood up, and now he was furious. His eyes blazed with righteous indignation.

"Henry, please!" Zoe said loudly. She stood up and stepped in front of him. Without realizing it, her hand went to his chest. "Please, listen to me. Please," She begged.

"What?" He asked.

"Do you trust me, Henry?"

And for what seemed like a far longer time than any clock could confirm, they stood facing each other, her hand upon his chest, their eyes not leaving the other's.

"Yes," he answered eventually.

"Then please do not look. One day you will know, but not now and not yet."

"You know who did it, don't you?"

"I do. And it'll only cause hurt and make things worse for you to know."

Henry looked as if he carried the weight of the world on

his shoulders, and she'd just told him that his replacement had been canceled.

"How can you be so confident that everything will work out fine?" He asked.

"I have to be. Because God is always in control, in the good times and the bad times," she answered truthfully. "I'm a bundle of nerves to be honest. I guess we both need the patience of Job to get us through this."

And that was all the motivation Henry needed. Hearing the Bible's wisdom, that his dad had referred to so many times, in the mouth of Zoe. Almost word for word, as his father had said.

She lowered her hand, and they both took their seats. They then spoke about Rachel and Robert, with Henry updating her.

When they finished, Henry remained in his study, but she brought a plate of lasagna and a greek salad to him for dinner. She took the boys to Jordan's room again and read to them, as was becoming the custom. She then prepared to leave for the evening. In the kitchen, as she was dishing some lasagna and salad into a bowl for herself, Stacie came in.

"Hey Zoe, I just saw Henry and he told me what happened. Carol is no favorite of mine. My brother doesn't see it but she's after him. Sorry you're caught up in the drama. How about we go out tomorrow after you drop the boys off. We can pamper ourselves and get our nails done. That will still leave you enough time to pick up the boys," Stacie said.

"Sure, I'd love that," Zoe responded.

"Cool, I'll meet you at the nail shop on Madison St. Are you familiar with that one?" Stacie questioned.

"I know exactly where it is. See you then," Zoe waved.

The next day when Zoe arrived at the shop, not only was Stacie there but Jessica as well.

"Hi Zoe, I'm Jessica. I couldn't miss the opportunity of a

girl's day seeing that I'll be on lockdown after this baby is born. I've heard so much about you from Stacie and the boys but they didn't tell me how pretty you are. I'm so happy Henry met you. He really needed the help," Jessica stated as she turned to Stacie and gave a huge smile. Seems they had a private mental conversation going.

"Let's get started. It's been too long since I've had a proper mani/pedi," Stacie complained.

As their feet soaked, Jessica was the first to start the conversation.

"So Zoe, seems like we were living very close to each other when we were younger but never met. Why did you move to New York?"

I moved here for nursing school. Once I was done with that, I began nursing full time and then finished my first year of med school." Zoe answered.

Jessica whipped her head around and stared at her.

"How do you go from med school to being a nanny. No offense but that's a definite change of careers. They're not even in the category?" Jessica questioned.

"It became overwhelming. All I ever did was work and study. I didn't have time for family and friends and when I realized that it wasn't what I wanted anymore, I left," Zoe answered but her voice had quieted down to a whisper.

There was a moment of awkward silence. Being the excellent reporter that Jessica was, she took the lead and changed the subject.

"Tell us about your family, Zoe. Our family is crazy. We're all over the place. Our brother William lives in Nashville but is always on tour. This is the longest I've seen Stacie stay in one place since I don't know when. Sometimes I forget I have a sister," Jessica laughed.

Zoe laughed, "My family is the typical family, mom, dad and my sister. My sister and I would do these fun days as well."

"I didn't know you had a sister. We should get together sometimes. Does she live in New York?" Stacie inquired.

Zoe mumbled, "she's in North Carolina with my parents."

Again, Jessica noticed a change in Zoe's attitude. A sadness.

"So how do you like working for Henry?" Jessica smiled.

"It's nice. He's so wonderful. He is such a good dad to the boys. He's so wonderful to his employees. He is always busy but always takes time out for the important things. He's just Mr. Wonderful. He pays attention to detail." Zoe was going on and on.

Stacie's voice rose. "Wait a minute. Are we talking about the same Henry? The one that forgot to hire a nanny, forgot to pick the boys up from school. The Henry that can't see the snake right in front of him until it bites him."

Jessica remarks, "Hey Stacie, I think she's got it bad."

Jessica and Stacie high five each other. They've been wanting Henry to meet someone. They knew Judith would approve. She wouldn't want Henry wasting away burying himself in work. The boys needed someone to give them the nurturing that they deserved. This would be good for the family. They couldn't wait to get on the phone with mom.

"No, it's not like that at all. We have a professional relationship, that's it. Henry doesn't see me like that. I'm just the nanny that cares for his kids," Zoe stammered.

"I think she's as blind as Henry is. We'll let them continue to think it's professional for now," Jessica told Stacie.

After they were done with their girl's day, Zoe went to pick up the boys and Stacie and Jessica had a late lunch.

"Jessica," Stacie asked, "Are your reporter ears tingling?"

"Yes, we're missing something. It may be nothing but did you see how sad and quiet she got when she talked about her family. Maybe the relationship is strained or something. I understand that it sometimes happens in families but when she told us about herself, she never mentioned her sister. What about med school? How do you go from med school to being a nanny? I can see her being a nurse or something else in the medical field but a nanny? Even though there is nothing at all wrong with the profession, something just doesn't seem right. I may have to use some of my resources to see what's going on with Zoe. The last thing we need is for Henry and the boys to get too attached and have to suffer another loss," Jessica responded.

That night as Zoe was leaving, Stacie stopped her to let her know how much she and Jessica had enjoyed her company. Stacie had wanted to know about her mother, what she was like, what she did for a living and whether they were close. Zoe revealed that her mother was a very strict woman who wanted the best for her and loved her dearly. She didn't always go about showing it the right way though. She was a postal worker, and they were close. And that was all she wanted to know.

Zoe had no idea she had unwittingly walked into a snare, which Stacie would soon spring.

CHAPTER 17

Dreams That Make Us Cry

ONE

Zoe woke early the next morning with Emma's anxious face staring down at her, startling her. As she sat up in her bed, she realized she was drenched with sweat.

"What?" She managed to say, her voice croaky and her throat dry.

"You were having some sort of nightmare," said Emma.

"Oh," was all she said.

"Yeah, and moaning and saying, 'no' over and over. Do you want to talk about it?" She asked.

The relationship between them had been somewhat strained this week, and not just because of her quitting the job Emma had gotten for her, but also because of her going back on the promise she had made to herself to never return to being a nanny. Emma didn't know any of the issues she was dealing with in the Stone's home but knew something was stressing her.

She looked at Emma and thought maybe a neutral voice

can add some wisdom. "Sure," she said, "Let me just freshen up. Make us some coffee?"

"I'm on it," Emma replied.

After she'd finished up in the bathroom and dressed, she headed to the kitchen, passing Bets' door, which was still closed.

"So, what nightmare got you all in a tizz this morning?"

Zoe remembered the key elements of the dream. She was driving a car, with Junior, Jordan, and Henry inside. And even though she was herself in the dream, she was also Judith, Henry's late wife. And then another car smashed into them, killing everyone except her, Zoe-Judith. The driver of the other car exited their vehicle and walked over to the wreck of a car they were all in, and the driver was laughing. When the driver pulled her door open and dragged her out, she eventually saw the face of the driver, which was when Emma had managed to wake her. In the dream and in reality, she'd been saying 'no' repeatedly after seeing the face of the laughing driver—it was her, not the Zoe-Judith amalgam, but Zoe alone. Telling the dream in full to Emma would have confused her more than answered questions, so Zoe simply said she'd been having a dream that the Stone family had died in an accident and she had been responsible. In a sense that *was* the point of the dream.

"That's insane," Emma responded. "Why do you think you had it? Is it due to how hard they're working and stressing you at the same time?"

She told Emma about *some* of the issues she'd been struggling with at work, the simple version—enough to paint a relatively clear picture of her dilemma and to hopefully allow Emma to give some advice. She told her that Henry was dealing with a major crisis at work that could bring about the end of his business, and about Carol and her jealousy. Emma listened quietly as her friend spoke, without interrupting. When Zoe finished, they sat in silence for a few moments.

"Well," Emma said. "That explains the look on your face every day."

"I guess," replied Zoe. "What do you think?"

"I think you'll thank me for agreeing with you and then probably slap me for pointing something out that I think you're missing."

"Okay," said Zoe, frowning with uncertainty.

"So, I agree, this Carol woman is trouble. And she needs to be dealt with. And I do hope Henry does as he has promised and puts her in her place. She's making things unmanageable for you in that apartment."

"Agreed."

"Yeah. And then the part you won't like, and from what you told me about Henry and the kids and especially the way you talk about them—Henry especially—you're playing with fire. Do not involve yourself in their business."

"What do you mean?"

"It's pretty plain to see you have the hots for Henry. But he is your boss, and clearly in over his head. He is vulnerable and you're attractive. I think you need to burn that bridge down now."

"I don't know what you—"

"Yeah, you do," insisted Emma. "You're not a fool, so don't pretend to be one. Either that man is going to use you for his pleasure, or you're going to use him for your pleasure, or you're both going to break each other's hearts. And you do not want that kind of drama."

Zoe was stunned at her friend's candor.

"Look, I'm not stupid. I can see and tell there's lots you've left out, and that's fine. Maybe you two have already been "together."

"Emma!" Zoe snapped. "You know I'd never—"

"Okay, okay," interrupted Emma. "Apologies. I know your whole virgin thing is important to you and your religion as well. I just mean you've not told me everything. You've left key bits out. And those key bits are the real problems in this situation. They're the reason you feel you're killing the family in your dreams."

Zoe stared in disbelief at her friend and how on target her observation was.

"Right, your face tells me I'm on the right path," Emma said. "So, I'm just filling in the blanks the best I know how. Apparently, I was wrong about the affair."

"Yes, you were," said Zoe.

"Something I don't think you're aware of though," said Emma, "I think it's part of the reason you're also walking around all week like a headless chicken. You said how busy and focused Henry is on work, and so you know in the back of your mind but are too afraid to bring it to the front of your mind."

"What?"

"He's neglecting his children. You can see it, but you're avoiding it because it means you will have to confront him about it and let's be honest, you avoid confrontations. Plus if you have the hots for him—"

"What? Are you..."? She was stunned. "That's nonsense!"

"What? The part that you avoid confrontations or the part about you believing Henry is neglecting his kids?"

"Henry is a good father. He loves those boys and does his best—"

"When he spares the time to be home?" She cut her off. "And even then, when not on his laptop, according to you, right?"

Zoe stared at her friend with incredulity.

"So, I'm right, and more so about being afraid of confrontation."

"I confronted Henry about Carol!" She fired back.

"I don't doubt that you did, even though it was only after he *asked* you to, but I agree. You do speak up. However, when it involves children and parents, then you don't."

"No," Zoe said softly, looking away as tears ran down her face.

"It was the same with that other family with the teenage older sister. You knew she was sneaking out to hang out with her friends, even though her parents had a strict curfew."

"Stop."

"And before that—"

"Stop!" shouted Zoe, slamming her fist on the kitchen table. Emma jumped in fright.

Once again they both sat in silence as Zoe composed herself, wiping away tears.

"I'm sorry," said Emma. "I'm not trying to hurt or upset you. I'm just trying to help you see a pattern behind your... choices."

"Do you really believe... all that you said about me?"

Emma nodded. "I've believed so for some time. You're my best friend. It's why I'm trying to steer you away from nanny work towards nursing. At least there you won't be in that situation with kids. You don't like kids being hurt. So even working in as a CPR instructor would be better."

"And you never said anything?"

"Honestly, I thought you knew and were just... I don't know, torturing yourself."

She was stunned. And it was true, at least that there was a pattern of looking after kids and wanting to avoid seeing the kids being hurt. *Did you really know that on some level though? Is that why you wanted to abandon childcare work?* It made sense, given what had happened to her parents and Chloe. "And so you think part of why I'm also stressed is because I want to tell Henry he's neglecting his kids, but am afraid to do so?"

"Okay, now that I think about it, the kids aren't in any real danger of having their feelings hurt by you confronting Henry. So then, I don't know. You seem more concerned about the kids' feelings than the parents, so unless you're breaking the pattern with Henry..." Emma paused. "Unless, you really do have the hots for him and want to avoid conflict 'cos you're scared of alienating him?"

Emma was of course right. She did want to avoid seeing kids getting hurt, but in this instance, she didn't want to see the kids *and* Henry being hurt. They were a package deal, in this instance. Because of that night five years ago. And because she did have feelings for Henry. And because Junior was in danger of being hurt.

Zoe sighed in frustration. And Henry was in danger of being an absent father.

"One more thing for me to deal with," she said pessimistically.

"No, I don't think you should involve yourself in that. Remember, Henry is not a friend, nor is he family. He's your boss. Do not involve yourself in your employer's business. It's why I'm also telling you to find someone else to crush on because you're making this job even more complicated than your previous nanny jobs."

"I appreciate your help, I really do. This was eye-opening for sure. But I disagree with you. I should have said something, regardless of the outcome. It was the right thing to do."

"Fine. You never listen when you set your mind on something, anyway. But I'll say this, the right thing isn't always the right thing for everybody."

CHAPTER 18

If You Fail to Plan

ONE

Henry yawned as he sat in the kitchen drinking coffee. Zoe would be arriving in the next 20 minutes or so, he suspected. He'd had very little sleep the night before, trying to find a solution to all the problems he had to deal with. He had to get Carol to back off from Zoe, and while that was probably the easiest problem in his life, it was strangely difficult for him to see himself doing. He needed to end the issues between Junior and Zoe, though she insisted on dealing with that herself. Stacie has been eerily quiet lately and missing in action a lot as well. And then, worst of all is the Robert Williams case. He had decided to use the man's true name. He believed that Rachel would come around and drop her suit against 2-b-frank. As Zoe reminded him, God was in control. And he should believe.

And so he had messaged Marshall ten minutes ago asking to meet ASAP. He considered adding to the text that he should not tell Jessica, but felt it was wrong of him to ask a man to lie to his wife, especially when the wife was his sister as well.

His phone beeped. Marshall had replied and suggested 8 AM at Chello's. He texted back that he would be there.

Stacie came downstairs five minutes later, surprising Henry, who was unaccustomed to seeing her up so early unless he'd asked her to mind the boys.

He'd told her about his discussion with Zoe, and so she knew everything.

"You're up early—" He began.

"Why are you meeting with Marshall?"

"Wow, that was quick."

"Why would he not tell Jessica?"

"It's not that," replied Henry, "... it's that—"

"That she told me?"

"Yeah."

"She called to ask me what's going on because you're being secretive again. Something is clearly going on with Robert Morgan and you're saying nothing."

Henry knew better than to argue or hide anything from Stacie.

"Yes, there is something. And no, I am not hiding anything. I was waiting until I had all the details and then I was going to tell the family, because contrary to popular opinion about me, I'm not trying to be a martyr and carry everything on my back," he scolded her.

"I see," said Stacie, taking a step back. "Okay then, sorry. When will you be—"

"Tonight. Is that fine?"

"Yes," replied Stacie. She continued looking at him, as though there was something else.

"What?" He asked.

It seemed to Henry that she was about to say something more when she shook her head. "Nothing. I'm heading back to bed." She turned and headed towards the stairs.

"Stacie."

She stopped and looked back at him.

"I love you."

"Yeah, yeah. Love you too, blah-blah-blah," she replied, smiling playfully.

~

Henry was in his bedroom dressing when he heard the lift opening.

Zoe, he groaned in his mind. He slapped his forehead. He hadn't yet spoken to Carol and needed to get to work to meet with Marshall.

He opted for texting Carol in the meantime. He asked if he could meet with her tonight regarding Zoe and indicated that she would remain working for him as his nanny, and he would explain why tonight. He mentioned that the talk tonight was serious and was about his and Carol's future.

Arriving downstairs, he relayed the details of his text message to Zoe, who herself seemed anxious and stressed. Without thinking he put his hand on her shoulder and asked if she was fine.

"Yes, I'm okay. It's just so many things happening at once." She smiled bravely, but thinly. She put her hand over his and squeezed. When she realized what she'd done, she pulled her hand away quickly. "I'm so sorry, Henry!"

Henry laughed. Looking into her beautiful and honest eyes, he suddenly felt free of the many burdens he was carrying, and full of light, hope, and happiness instead.

"It's okay, Zee," he replied.

She smiled back at him. "Zee?"

"It suits you I think," and then he did something that took them both by surprise, he gently tapped the tip of her nose with his index finger.

"Um... okay," she said, laughing nervously, but to Henry, the light in her eyes had swelled to fullness.

"I have to run," he said.

"Then run, H, run!" She said.

As he walked past her to the lift foyer, he was laughing and shaking his head vigorously. "Not on your life, 'H.' Anything but that!"

As the lift doors closed, both Henry and Zoe noticed Junior standing in the dining room, having heard the entire exchange.

"Hey, my man! How are things going with you?" Henry asked as he sat down with Marshall at Chello's.

"Surviving, Dude. Your sister has graduated from being pregnant to being dangerous when not fed."

"Aah," laughed Henry. "She always liked to eat!"

"So, what's up? I must confess to being concerned because Jessica is concerned. Dad called yesterday to say you've not updated him about the Morgan case, and then Stacie was called and she apparently knows nothing."

"Yeah, I heard. I got the third degree from Stacie this morning."

"People are just concerned about you, Dude."

"Yeah, I know. I just wanted to wait until I had the full picture and knew the level of threat I'm dealing with before I come to the family."

"Level of threat?" Marshall asked, looking worried. "Henry, what happened?"

"When you know what happened, believe me, you'll know I need help. This is beyond me."

He told his brother-in-law about Robert Williams, the cyber-hacker. He had received confirmation that Robert Morgan was indeed Robert Williams and the criminal record was legit.

"Henry, that's crazy!" Marshall said. "I can't believe such a thing could have happened. How would he have been able to gain access remotely? It's not like the firewall can't be bypassed, but remotely, it's virtually impossible." Marshall sat back, a thought had occurred to him. "Wait, did he have his phone with him at your hearing?"

"Yes, he did. He asked if he could record the hearing."

Marshall nodded. "That's how he did it. It's the same way he accessed Rachel's phone, through his mobile device."

Henry slapped his forehead. "I allowed him to do it!"

"Don't stress. Who would have thought he'd be so shrewd? It's beyond crazy. What can I do to help?"

"A few things, I hope. Can you help in any way to retrieve our data and the pictures of Rachel, and how do we go about beefing up security, and have a better employee screening system in place?"

"Yes to all three," said Marshall. "We can beef up security and the screening process easily. Having said that, there is really little to enhance your screening software. Most of it is third-party vetting. I got you the top-tier programs anyway."

"Okay."

"The fact that Williams dodged that vetting is more testimony to his skills at cybercrime, than any defects in the screening process."

"Right, I'm with you."

"The firewall and other redundancies I can definitely bolster. I can literally put you on par with banking security software."

"That sounds good," Henry said. "And what about tracking him and getting our data back? I need to have an answer for him before he feels he needs to make an example. Either we bury the case against him and we survive or we go to the cops and he buries us instead."

"You said that Rachel won't cease her suit against him anyway, so you're pretty much without a choice really."

"There is that, yes," he agreed. A thought occurred to him, as a plan began taking shape in his mind. "Do you know how that phone hacking device works?"

"Yes, why?"

"Can you make one yourself?"

"Yes, of course. What's going on in your head?" Marshall asked, intrigued.

Henry told him his plan.

"Let me bring in my best guys and we'll see what happens," he said, excitedly. I can't promise it'll happen the way you think, but I can promise to give you what you need and do our best."

CHAPTER 19

All the Pieces Are on the Board

ONE

With Marshall and several his staff setting up at 2-b-frank and needing to access their servers and terminals, Henry decided to give everyone the day off.

Next, he called his parents and explained the situation to them. He apologized for keeping it from them but explained that he felt it important to first get as many of the details as possible, confirm those details, and then try and have a plan of action in place. He believed that with Marshall involved, that plan was coming to fruition, and he was very optimistic about its results. Fred and Linda were understandably concerned, but grateful that Henry had not kept this from them. They prayed over the telephone for God's help, guidance, and blessings.

Next, he arranged a video call with Jessica, Stacie, and William, and relayed the same message to them. The outcome was essentially the same as when he had spoken to their parents.

He was about to leave the office when he received a text

message from his mother. His father was packing his bags and would be flying through later that day. She asked if he could collect him at LaGuardia. Henry was both relieved knowing his father was on the way, but also anxious for the same reason.

TWO

Zoe had just arrived back at the apartment and was busy doing the breakfast dishes when the lift beeped, opened, and Carol walked in.

"Selma!" She called from the lift foyer.

Zoe went to meet her.

"My name is Zoe," she said.

"Yes," said Carol. "Mister Stone says that I can use you when I need. I need a maid to clean up on a daily basis. Two hours a day should be enough time for a strong worker like you to get my apartment looking spic and span."

"No, thank you. If you need someone to clean on a daily basis, it sounds like you need a maid and that I am not," Zoe replied firmly.

"I see. Obviously, I'll pay you."

"It's still a no."

"And here I thought some extra cash would be just what you'd be after."

"I'm a nanny, not a maid," answered Zoe, coolly.

Smiling, Carol looked around at the neatly cleaned and tidied place. "Are you sure? The house has never been cleaner. Working for me would give you more experience on your resume."

Zoe tried to hide her surprise.

"Carol, you don't know me but let me introduce myself. I graduated at the top of my class from college, summa cum laude. I can't count the amount of times I was named employee of the month when I was a nurse at the hospital. I applied and was accepted into the top med school in the country. What I do today is a choice, not a necessity. All your little comments only prove to me how insecure of a woman you are. The games you play are for children not a grown woman," Zoe spoke.

"I say this not to brag but just to inform you that I have options. So please don't think that I don't. I'm here because Henry asked me to be. Nothing more or nothing less," Zoe stated.

Carol's mouth stood open and she was speechless. It took her a moment to recover.

"Well, suit yourself," said Carol. "I'm sure there are other more grateful folks out there who would be happy to earn something extra."

"I'd suggest you make your offer to them, yes. That would be a kindness you can do."

Smiling contemptuously at her, Carol left the apartment.

Henry needs to talk to this she-devil, thought Zoe. *The mischief she is causing is not good.*

Junior had nothing but dirty looks for her this morning, and she was sure Carol was behind that. That and many other things.

THREE

Still at the office, Henry went down to Chello's to grab a coffee and a bagel. He would head home after and have his talk with Carol. As he left the cafe, Robert Williams blocked his path.

"Hello, Henry. How're things going?" He smirked.

"Robert. What are you doing here?"

"Just checking up on you. Looking good, like you've lost weight. Stress getting to you?"

"I have nothing to say to you," Henry said, stepping past him.

Robert blocked his path again. "Always did like your no-nonsense attitude. So, let me get to the point. Have your brother-in-law and his goons removed from 2-b-frank. Immediately."

"Or what?"

"Don't be daft, Henry." Robert laughed. "You know what. I'll dump all your sensitive client data on the internet. Also, I want your reply by tomorrow morning at 9 AM or those files will see the light of a billion computers the world over." He took Henry's coffee and bagel out of his hand and walked away, whistling pleasantly.

Henry went upstairs and told Marshall everything that had just happened. Ten minutes later, Marshall and all his staff exited the Bremicker Building.

FOUR

Stacie was about to lie down when Henry called, asking if she could come to the office, pick up his car, and then drive to LaGuardia to fetch dad.

She found Zoe in the lift foyer, getting ready to fetch the boys. They always ended early on a Wednesday. She explained briefly that she would be leaving soon herself, but just wanted to make a quick sandwich.

As Zoe entered the lift, she called to her.

"By the way, which Post Office did your mom work in?" she asked. "Was it the one in Newhill?"

"Yes," said Zoe.

"And she's still there to this day, or retired?"

"She... passed sadly," said Zoe. "I need to leave, Stacie. Otherwise, I'll be late for the boys."

"Of course," said Stacie, smiling at her.

Ensnared, thought Stacie.

FIVE

Arriving at the school, Zoe waited by the car, certain that Carol would not try anything today. After the bell rang, she saw Jordan coming out and collected him. She waited for Junior, but he wasn't coming out. She was about to enter the gate to search when a teacher came up to her.

"You're Zoe, yes?" asked the teacher.

"Yes, I am," she smiled back.

"I'm Sharon. Junior is in last period with me for Physics, and I've kept him behind for 30 minutes to finish his work, as he was refusing to do so during class. I'd have been here sooner to tell you—apologies for that. I had to wait for my class assistant to get back from the toilet."

Zoe thanked the teacher and asked if she and Jordan could wait inside the school for Junior, which was fine.

When Junior did emerge, he saw Zoe, scowled at her, and walked past her. Zoe went up to him and asked him politely to walk with her and Jordan. He then walked faster, to get ahead of her. Reaching for him, she took hold of his hand.

"Junior, I do not want to have to tell your dad how naughty you are, or that you're being rude to me. Already your dad is unhappy about your behavior, but I told him that you're a good boy, and will listen to me. So, I expect that. Am I clear?"

"Yeah," he said.

"So please walk with Jordan and me. I only want to help you and be your friend. Nothing more. I promise."

"Sure," he replied. It worried her how agreeable he seemed to be. As they entered and crossed the parking lot, he suddenly wrenched his hand free, and ran across the lot in front of the teachers and other parents.

Turning his head to look at her, he shouted at the top of his voice, "You'll never be my friend, and you're not my mommy. You're a bad person!"

As Zoe watched and reached a hand towards him, she saw a car driving towards him. In that second, she saw the driver looking next to them, at their child in the passenger seat. Neither Junior nor the driver were aware of each other.

"Junior stop!" She screamed at the top of her voice, but she knew it would be too late. Letting go of Jordan's hand, she ran towards Junior, turned her head towards Jordan, and shouted, "Don't move!" to him.

Crashing into Junior, she knocked him out of the way, as the car hit her instead.

SIX

As Henry entered the apartment his cell phone rang. Looking at the display, he saw it was the school. When he answered, he learned that there had been an accident at the school.

The boys were fine, which he was extremely grateful for, just a little traumatized, but Zoe had been injured after a car knocked her over. She'd been taken to NYP by one of the teachers. Henry immediately hailed an Uber, and when it arrived, headed to the school to collect his boys.

CHAPTER 20

When the Dam Bursts

ONE

Whened Henry arrived at the school, he was directed straight to the principal's office. The minute he entered, the boys ran into his arms. They had been sitting calmly and quietly on the couch, but when they were in his arms, they both burst into tears.

"Are you guys okay? Jordie? Buddy?" He asked.

Both boys replied that they were. The principal was Ronald Golberg, and he asked to speak privately with Henry. One of the teachers sat with the boys, while they spoke in the waiting room.

Ronald expressed his concern, having heard of the altercation the previous day between Zoe and Carol, and how Junior had then also apparently been running freely in the parking lot, without supervision. When Henry inquired as to what precisely had happened, Ronald explained the order of events that led to Zoe being run over.

"You're saying that Junior pulled free of Zoe, ran into the

lot towards an oncoming vehicle, and then Zoe was knocked over saving him?"

"It would seem so, yes. If not for her, I fear that Junior might have been far more severely injured than a few bruises on his knees."

"But if not for him in the first place, none of this would have happened."

"That's one way of looking at it, Mister Stone. Another is to consider what might have prompted the lad to do so in the first place. There is some unhappiness, perhaps even frustration somewhere along the way that's prompting this type of behavior. Perhaps that's where you should focus your efforts."

Henry left the school with the boys. Satisfied that they were both okay, they took an Uber to NYP hospital. Along the way, he called Stacie to tell her about Zoe's accident. She had just collected their father and was about to leave the airport. She found his report of the incident at the school to be disturbing. He asked if they could swing by the hospital to collect the boys, while he checked on Zoe, to which she agreed.

In the car, he felt it best not to discuss what had happened with the boys. He was too traumatized himself, and angry, and thought he would say the wrong thing. Too many things were piling on top of him, Carol, Robert, Zoe, Rachel, and now this.

When they arrived at the hospital, he was happy to see Stacie and his father waiting for them at the entrance. Everyone embraced in a great big family hug, and then Henry caught everyone up as best as he could. He felt it best to leave out Junior's indiscretion, though he could tell both his father and Stacie could read between the lines. They offered to wait for him until he was done, but he suggested they rather head home with the boys.

When he arrived in Zoe's room, she was propped up on the bed with a neck brace and a sling on her right arm. The arm was also bandaged around the elbow.

"Hey!" She shouted a little too loudly. She appeared very happy to see Henry, who came towards her. He wanted to come to her right side, but then all the bandages detoured him to her left instead. Taking her hand in his, she squeezed before he could.

"Are the boys okay? And are you okay?" She asked him, a little slurry.

"Wait, you're in the hospital, all bandaged up and you're asking if we're okay?"

She giggled. "I'm on such lovely meds, my darling Henry. Wait, let me call the nurse quickly." She reached for the remote with the call button. She pushed it repeatedly, and so Henry took it from her.

"Are you in pain, can I do anything?" He asked worriedly.

"No, my love, why would you think so?" She slurred back.

He looked at her, unsure of how to respond. He was worried about her.

Seeing the worry, she placed her hand on his cheek, "It's okay, Darling. The nurse will be here soon. They're very prompt. Emma threatened them!"

"But what is wrong? Do you need anything? Can I get anything for you?"

"You are soooo cute when you worry, did you know that?" She asked and released his hand, just as a petite nurse with a long blonde plait walked in.

"What is all this fuss about, Zoe?" She demanded.

"He needs drugs!" whispered Zoe, pointing her finger at Henry.

"Ah, you must be Henry," said the nurse.

"Yes. Do I know you?" he asked.

"No, but you know my roomie who is over the top from the pain meds they gave her, which means I know you."

"Oh, you're one of her roommates," said Henry.

"He's the one I'm marrying!" said Zoe, thinking she was still whispering. She held a hand next to her mouth so that Henry wasn't supposed to see her mouth, except she was blocking the wrong side of her mouth.

"I see," said Emma, smiling.

Henry blushed, turning red.

"Isn't he gorgeous?" Zoe asked.

"Quite," agreed Emma, smiling at Henry.

"I probably should wait outside until she... uh..." he stuttered.

"Yeah, that might be good," agreed Emma. "In fact, this'll be knocking her out for a good few hours. Why not come back this evening?"

"I see," said Henry, walking out of the room. He turned to have a last look at Zoe and saw Emma following behind.

"Aww, sweet, man," she said.

"Uh, what is?"

"A last longing look to tide you until tonight," she cooed.

"Oh... uh... I'm not..."

"She's fine, just badly banged up" Emma winked. "Badly dinged, should I say?" She giggled. "Mostly muscle bruising, no breaks or fractures. She'll be in some heavy pain for a few days, and stiff as a board, but I'm sure she'll be okay in your care."

Henry was home again within the hour. He had to deal with Carol, Junior, and Marshall. Stacie was busy making dinner and his father was in the lounge with the boys. When he entered the kitchen, Stacie asked how Zoe was and was happy to know that she wasn't as bad as they initially thought.

She again looked like there was something she wanted to say, but then she sent him through to the lounge to let dad and the boys know.

What's that about? Henry wondered as he went to the lounge.

When Dad and the boys heard Zoe was okay, they were all relieved, Junior especially, who burst into tears. Dad suggested that he take the boy to the balcony and they talk. Henry nodded.

"Buddy," he called gently to Junior, who looked up at him. "Don't you want to come and sit with me outside?"

Junior nodded shyly.

On the balcony, they sat at the patio table, under the umbrella which stood in the center. Stacie popped out quickly, with two glasses of lemonade and ice. She kissed both father and son on the forehead and then went back inside.

"I'm very upset and unhappy, Junior. I'm really doing my best to be calm and not lose my temper. So please don't lie or hide anything. I'm giving you the chance, to be honest and to tell the truth. There's much that I already know, believe me. I just want to hear you tell the truth."

He nodded, but couldn't look his father in the eye, but looked at the ground.

"Firstly, have you been talking to Aunt Carol about Zoe?"

He nodded his head.

"And what have you been saying?"

"Aunt Carol says Zoe is a bad woman, and she's trying to take mommy's place. And that if we show you we don't like her, you'll send her away."

"Did you or Carol change the settings for the lift?"

"She showed me on her lift what to do. And then I did it to our lift," he said, still looking at the ground.

146

"Okay. And who's idea was it to not listen to Zoe in the school parking lot?"

He sat silently.

"Junior?"

"It was mine." He burst out crying. Heart-wrenching sobs escaped the boy. Henry grabbed him and hugged him fiercely.

When Junior had settled a bit, Henry faced him with both hands on his shoulders.

"What you did was not nice, but I understand why you did it. Zoe is not going to replace your mom, she doesn't want to do that. She's really just trying to take care of us all. She cares for us and wants what's best for us. She cares for you too. She jumped in front of a car for you. That's how much she cares."

He nodded and burst into tears again.

"She wants to be your friend, you just need to let her. Please... stop listening to Carol. That's the real person who caused Zoe to get hurt today. Can you see that? She actually tried to hurt Zoe, using you. She's been interfering and making you think badly of Zoe. Carol will no longer be allowed in the apartment, and you're not to have contact with her. Is that clear?"

"Yes, Daddy."

"Sometimes in life, people that seem good can actually be very bad. And sometimes, they're so bad that they want other people—other good people, like you—to do bad things with them. You need to be very careful of such people."

"Is Aunt Carol one of those really bad people?"

"It's never nice to speak badly of people, but Jesus does tell us in the Bible, that you will know good and bad people by their fruits."

"Fruits?" Junior asked.

"Yes, like a tree can only have good or bad fruit, but not both. In the same way, the things people do or say, will either be good, or bad. And that means when someone does something bad, you *can* say, 'That was a bad thing they did,' and maybe they're actually bad people too."

"So Carol is a bad person?"

"I think she did some bad things. And how she responds when I talk to her, will show if she is a good person who just did some bad things or an actual bad person. Like you're a good person, who did a bad thing. But I know you're good because you feel bad and you told the truth."

"Yes, Daddy."

"Just don't ever do that again."

"No, Daddy."

Henry hugged him tightly.

"I love you, Buddy," He said.

"I love you too, Dad."

≈

Henry felt as though he were ticking off checkboxes. Junior was done, and now it was Carol's turn.

Entering the lift, he pushed the button for Carol's apartment. Barely a minute later, the doors opened and Carol stood in her foyer, wearing a short but tight skirt, and a cleavage-baring blouse. "Henry, dear. Do come in."

Stepping into the foyer, he greeted her.

"Well, hello yourself, you look so dapper today."

"I won't be long, Carol. I just came from the hospital."

"Oh, dear!" She said, immediately looking concerned. "What happened?"

"I don't know if you're being sincere or not, but Zoe was knocked over in the parking lot at school, trying to reign in Junior. It seems someone has been prodding him to dislike her and to make things difficult for her. Like changing the settings for the lift, so she couldn't get into the apartment."

"Good Lord, Henry. That's awful. That poor child."

"She's not a child, Carol, she's barely a few years younger than you and I."

"I just mean, she should be more focused when walking—"

"Really? Are we going to pretend that neither of us knows the truth? I knew before Junior told me, Carol."

"Whatever he's told you, he's mistaken." She laughed as though it should have been obvious.

"A ten-year-old child knows how to reprogram the lift's *Night Security*?"

"The kids of today, Henry."

"Carol. Let me be frank with you. I have no romantic interest in you. I never have and never will. I should have spoken to you days ago about this but didn't. And because of that, an amazing woman is in the hospital now. You played mind games with my son. For that, I've lost all respect for you. Please keep your distance from me and my family, and that includes Zoe because whether you like it or not, she is a part of t." Henry turned around and pushed the button for the lift, which opened immediately.

Stepping into the lift, he pushed the button for his apartment on the inside. "Goodbye Carol."

She stared at him with a blank expression as the doors closed.

CHAPTER 21

Love and all Things Squishy

ONE

When Henry arrived in the evening to visit Zoe, he had Stacie with him. When he walked into her room, she was happy and excited to see him, and then Stacie followed after him. When she saw Stacie and the look on her face, she knew what was afoot and her heart sank.

"Hi there," she said, more to Stacie than to Henry.

"Hi there. How are you?" answered Henry.

"I was okay. Until now."

Stacie gave nothing away facially. Henry looked puzzled though.

"Ladies?" He asked, looking from one to the other.

"That's why you came, isn't it?" Zoe asked.

"Yes, before things get out of hand. I'm sorry for what happened to you, with all my heart, but this is serious. And you need to explain yourself."

Henry was even more puzzled. "Stacie, what's gotten into you? This is—"

"It's okay Henry. I've never lied, not to you or any of your family."

"But you're guilty of some very serious omissions, though," Stacie corrected.

"What's going on?" He asked.

"Tell him what you know," Zoe invited Stacie.

Stacie nodded and took a deep breath. "Zoe is the eldest daughter of Charles and Diane Carlson, and the sister of Chloe Carlson. Her family perished in the accident with Judith. Zoe was born Zoe Carlson, but was taken in by her aunt and uncle, and then changed her surname to James, their surname."

Henry looked at his sister, and then at Zoe. "No, that's not possible."

Zoe, sighed as tears ran down her cheeks. "It's true, Henry. Everything she said is true."

"No!" He said again.

"It's true. I struggled to get her details on public record, but I used a contact that does tracing for me and found her details by tracking her mother through the US Postal Service. I double-checked. She was at Judith's funeral."

Henry dropped into a chair next to the bed.

"This is true?" He asked.

"Yes," replied Zoe.

"That's why I was drawn to you... because a part of me recognized you," he said. "Not because of..." He paused. "... not because of any other reason."

"Can you explain yourself?" asked Stacie.

Zoe opened her mouth to speak, but Henry got up and walked out of the room.

"Henry!" She shouted after him, but he was gone, leaving her alone with Stacie. "I never meant to hurt anyone."

"I don't know what to believe, but what I do know is that lying is never the way to prove that."

"I didn't lie. I just kept quiet so that I could..." She paused.

"So that you could what?" asked Stacie.

"It doesn't matter anymore. What I wanted most is now lost forever." She looked away towards the window. Stacie could see the tears pouring down her cheek.

"I'm sorry, Zoe. I like you, and that's what makes this so awful. I like you and I think Henry was falling for you. I had to do this before he and those boys got hurt. I don't know what you were trying to achieve by lying, but I had to put an end to it. Goodbye, Zoe," Stacie said and left the room.

TWO

Henry was really in no mood, but that evening after he arrived home, Marshall and Jessica arrived. By then, everyone knew the truth about Zoe.

Marshall was especially excited to see Henry.

"I have some news for you, Dude. Sorry about Zoe, but I have something that will cheer you up, I think."

He sat next to Henry at the dining table and took out his laptop. Opening the lid, the screen exited standby mode and hummed to life. Henry looked and immediately recognized the files as the companies.

"What the...?" He asked incredulously. "How is that possible?"

"It worked. When we flushed Robert out, and he made contact with you, the phone I gave you hacked his own phone and gave us access to his system."

"What do you mean, 'When you flushed him out?'" Dad stood in the doorway, looking very unhappy.

"We figured that Robert was watching Henry and the company, or monitoring them at least. So we came up with a plan. We would hack his system the way he had Rachel's and 2-b-franks, but we couldn't just approach him, or he'd catch on. So we had to let him come to us," explained Marshall.

"So, you set a trap to bait him? How?"

"We had Marshall and his crew come to the office to try to resolve the issues, knowing that Robert would see and not be happy," Henry explained. "And so he reached out to me almost immediately. Marshall created a phone that could hack Robert's system, and I kept it in my pocket. And it worked."

"Yep. Every file has been retrieved, including all of Rachel's. I deleted all his files, but tracked his online activity, creating a record, for the police. So we can still hand over our files and there's nothing he can do. And we have proof of his activity."

Henry and Marshall high-fived each other.

"And how dangerous was this plan?" Dad asked, clearly irritated. "What if Robert had a firearm? What if he tried to hurt you? What about your boys?"

"Dad, I'd never have gone ahead, if I hadn't gotten confirmation that Robert wasn't a violent offender. He's a harmless cybercriminal and bully. I promise you."

Dad sighed, and continued, "At least it's over. Just don't ever do something so reckless again. Either of you, am I clear?"

"Yes, sir," said both Henry and Marshall in unison.

THREE

Two days later, Henry met with Rachel to update her. The case file for Robert Williams had been handed over to the police. All her private material had been retrieved as well as the company files. Rachel was happy and proceeded with her civil case against Robert. She also agreed to drop the suit against 2-b-frank.

Stacie headed back to her career and moved out of Henry's spare room. Frank stayed another week with Henry, helping out with the boys and smoothing things over with the police.

He also spent the week at the office, helping to restore a sense of normalcy.

Henry ended up hiring a new nanny, Amelia Harcourt. She was good, but she was no Zoe.

FOUR

A month later, Junior came into Henry's bedroom one evening. He moaned that he missed how Zoe would read to them, making different voices for different characters and all her sound effects.

Henry admitted that he missed Zoe quite a lot himself. Junior said that he actually wished Zoe was there. She actually did cook pretty awesome and was pretty funny and fun, he said.

That night, Henry realized that he didn't just miss Zoe, he yearned for her. He couldn't sleep at night, he hardly ate, and his days felt empty and hollow. The spark that he felt when Zoe was in the room was gone. It was the same for the boys, especially Jordie. The sadness in him reminded Henry of Junior when Judith had died.

Carol, he saw occasionally, but she ignored him when he did. And he didn't mind.

Rachel returned to 2-b-frank that month but worked remotely. She still felt very uncomfortable with the fact that her colleagues had seen her in such a state of undress. Henry was just happy having her back at work. The case against Robert Williams was brought to court that month as well.

∼

The following week, Stacie threatened Henry over a video call.

"If you don't find out about her, then I disown you." She said.

"You were the one who exposed her as a fraud and now you want me to go running after her to ask her... to ask her what exactly?"

"For one, why she kept that from you, for another, whether she misses you as much as you miss her. It's so irritating and annoying, my annoyingly irritating Big Bro. You're like one of those hideously cute puppies with big eyes and sad faces all the time. And if it's not you that I gotta hear sob stories from, it's Junior. How he misses Zoe. Or Jordan."

"I don't—"

"Don't even go there, Bro! Every single time I call, you turn the convo to Zoe. Just reach out and call her. Maybe there was a valid reason for what she did. You owe yourself and the boys that much."

≈

A week later, Henry called Zoe, and she agreed to meet. She was working at Gina's again and agreed to meet the next day at Chello's.

FIVE

Zoe had been working for Tony again for the last two months. She had made a full recovery since her injuries. Henry had given her a very generous severance package. Three months' salary, and an email requesting that she have no further contact with him or the family. She had respected his wishes.

Emma, who had met him, was sad, as she had liked Henry. There was something very noble about him. Zoe tried to explain that it was because he was a Christian, but she was still resistant to that truth. At least a little.

Life had returned to normal for Zoe, and her daily routine was a happy one. Despite that, however, she did miss Henry and the boys, and not a day went by where she never thought of them and wondered what they were doing.

Many times she had considered reaching out to see if they were well, but thought that she should respect Henry's wishes, and didn't. And so it came as a great surprise when Henry reached out to her and asked to meet. She agreed and they settled on Chello's the next day.

SIX

When Henry arrived at Chello's, Zoe was already seated and sipping a coffee. When he saw her, he had to do everything in his power to stop himself from running to her and hugging her. He was that happy to see her.

When she saw him, she too felt the same rush and thrill to see him. Unlike him, she was less able to restrain herself and so as he approached, she hopped off her seat and came forward smiling. She was about to embrace him when she managed to reign in her emotions.

"How are you?" She asked instead, as they both sat.

"I'm good. You look good," he said.

"Thank you, so do you."

"Have you fully recovered?" He asked.

"Yeah. I have, thanks."

"Okay," He sighed. "Let me be blunt. I feel like there's this sword hanging over us that needs to be dealt with before we can... I don't know what. Let me take a page from you and be frank and open with you. I'm sorry for cutting you off. You got knocked over saving Junior and I treated you like... well, not in a nice way."

"I kept something vital from you, so I can understand that. How is he though? I miss him and Jordan terribly. I hope you weren't too hard on him. He didn't know any better. He was under the influence of a very conniving woman."

"He's fine. I wasn't too hard, but I think you would have done better. He misses you, you know?"

"Really?"

"Very much, yes. He realizes his mistake."

"That makes two of us."

"Can you tell me why?"

She sighed.

"For so long I believed that I killed my family. I ran away that night. They were on the road looking for me. I was a stupid child who had a mother who didn't always take kindly to independent thought. I wasn't keen on being a doctor, and she wanted me to be a doctor. So on my finals of my first year of med school, I'd had enough, threw a tantrum, called her terrible names, and ran out the house."

"Oh," said Henry.

"When I eventually got home a few hours later, the police were there. I thought for me. Well, I guess they were there for me. But not because I'd run away. They were there to inform me of what had happened."

"I'm sorry Zoe, that you lived with that burden for so many years. Terrible choices can sometimes result in terrible consequences, but the choices are never forced. Your parents did what they thought was right not because of you, regardless of you running away. It was the same with me. Judith was out that night blowing off steam. We'd had an argument and she went for a drive and never came home."

Zoe stared into his eyes and recognized that they were kindred spirits. "I didn't know that, Henry."

"No one knows besides me, and now you. So, I'm telling you that I know how you feel. I felt my wife's death was my doing too. But these are the circumstances, choices, and paths that are pre-determined for us all."

"Yes, that's it. God uses these horrible events and tragedies to bring about good."

"And what good came of your wife and my family's deaths?"

"I honestly don't know that yet, but maybe you and I are meant to find that out together?"

"Do you think so, Henry?"

"It depends on why you kept all this from me. No relationship can ever be established that's built on deceit. You need to have a really good reason."

She sighed. "How could I ever make up for causing my parents' death? I could never. But I promised God that I would make right what I had caused. That's why I worked for so many years with kids. And when I saw you in the streets all those times, it was like seeing someone I knew. It was only at the class, when you told me about yourself, that I figured out why I knew you. Because I saw you at the funeral five years ago. I saw your pain and I knew then what to do. I could never make things right for my family because they were gone, but I could make things right for Judith's family. I could keep my promise to God."

"And that's why you changed your mind about working as a nanny? So that you could make amends for that night five years ago?"

"Yes."

"And that's the only reason for keeping this from us? From me?" Henry asked.

"Yes, but I would have told you."

"But when?"

"Quite soon actually, Henry. I couldn't stand keeping this from you and your family."

"Why? What made you want to tell me?"

"Do you promise not to think badly of me?"

"I promise."

"I wanted to tell you because I was falling in love with you and the boys."

Epilogue

ONE YEAR LATER

Zoe woke up to the sounds of birds and the sun shining brightly. Today is her big day. She is becoming Mrs. Henry Stone. Everything she couldn't have imagined had taken place. She got her acceptance letter to return to med school and had completed orientation. After Henry proposed to her, they went and bought a house which can easily be called an estate. The Stone family had welcomed her with open arms after they called a family meeting in North Carolina. All the family heard and understood her reasoning behind her coming into Henry's and the boys' lives. They all went over to her hometown and visited her family and placed flowers on their graves. Zoe couldn't have asked for more. God's grace and mercy are abundant.

"Wake up sleepy head. Let's get this day started. This is all I've heard about for the last 6 months. Wedding this and wedding that, for someone who's getting married today, you sure are reluctant to come out of this room," William screamed as he banged on the door.

Zoe had gained a whole new family. A mom and dad, a brother who is a #1 recording artist, and 2 award winning reporters as sisters. Not to mention, the love of her life and two amazing sons. What more could she ask for.

Frank was so touched when Zoe asked him to give her away. He and Lisa were adamant that they have the wedding at their home. Lisa and the girls had done most of the work. They asked Zoe all her favorites and they took it from there.

As the girls were getting dressed, Junior and Jordan knocked on the door. Jessica answered and the boys stepped in.

"Zoe is it possible that we have a word with you in private?" Junior asked.

"Absolutely," Zoe nodded. "Could everyone excuse us for a moment."

Every one left but they all stood outside the door to listen.

"We love you and we couldn't ask for a better mother," Jordan stated.

Zoe began to cry because this was the first time they had called her mom.

"We know that you are marrying our dad, and we are happy about that, but we have something to ask you too," Junior said.

They both dropped down on one knee.

"Will you be our mommy for real? Daddy gave us this paper and said if you sign it, it means that you will be our mommy for real," Jordan explained.

Zoe pulled the boys into a hug.

"Junior, are you ok with this? I want you to know that I'd never try to take your mother's place. I'm ok with just being Zoe."

"But you're not just Zoe. I love you. Dad and I had a long talk. He told me that my 1st mommy will always be my mom. I got lucky. Where most people get one mommy, I got two. More people to love Jordie and me," Junior remarked.

"I just have one question," Zoe said to Junior. "Do you have a pen?"

Everyone rushed in the door and it was one big group hug with tears.

"Ok, everyone, it's time to get out. We have a wedding to finish getting ready for," Lisa said.

Four hours later at the altar, Henry, Zoe, Junior, and Jordan said, "I do!"

After the reception, Henry Stone and his family left for Italy. They decided to do a family honeymoon because Zoe had just gained a new family and she wasn't letting anyone of them out her sight.

As Henry fell asleep on the plane, he slips back into his familiar dream.

Henry runs and keeps looking back. Everything around him brings back childhood memories of him and his siblings running around playing hide and seek. This is different. Someone is chasing him. He's running as fast as he can, but his attacker is getting closer and closer.

Henry falls and throws his hands up in defense and yells, "Help! I don't know what you want but please don't hurt me."

A blinding light flashes before him and out of the spotlight comes Judith reaching for him.

She lightly responds, "Henry don't worry, I'm here. You are brave and strong, now get up. I'll never leave you. You can do this."

Henry grabs her hand. He just wants to hold on. "I can't do this without you. What if I fail?" Henry questions.

Life is meaningless without Judith. He grabs her hand once more and she allows him. For a moment they sit and hold hands. Judith begins to fade away but just before she vanishes, he looks down at her hands and notices that it's no longer Judith's hands he's holding, but a darker version of hers. He looks into her face puzzled and she smiles as she slowly drifts away.

Then there is a flash. He sees Judith walking towards him, and she once again places her hands in his. As he looks at their hands enclosed, Judith removes her right hand briefly. She places her hand back in his but this time the hand is the same dark shade it was moments ago. This is different. Why is one hand light and the other is dark. He looks up and Zoe is standing there with Judith. Judith removes her left had and replaces it with Zoe's other hand. As Zoe is holding hands with Henry, Judith smiles and quietly walk away.

Henry is startled awake. He gets it. Judith was telling him that it was ok for him to move on and that she approved of Zoe. Henry reached over and grabbed Zoe's hand and gave it a gentle kiss.

Zoe looked at him and they both mouthed the words, "I love you."

～

The very next day, the remainder of the Stones were having brunch on the deck. Lisa looked at Frank.

"Darling, two down and two to go. Who do you think is next?" Lisa asked.

William and Stacie looked at each other and laughed.

"Not me, Stacie. It must be you. I have a new tour starting. I'm much too busy," William teased.

"Couldn't be me. I'm on my way out of town tomorrow to cover a piece on the events unfolding in the Ukraine," Jessica smirked.

Love has a way of finding us when we least expect it," Frank pointed out.

Saving Her

If you loved Henry and Zoe's story, you will love "Saving Her." See Marshall's fight to save Jessica from the nightmare she lived everyday. Click here to go to the beginning of the Stone saga.

https://dl.bookfunnel.com/3xm87t2ujr

Made in the USA
Middletown, DE
29 March 2022

63368874R00102